D0300675

Praise for *The First Thing You See*

'This smart romantic comedy is charmingly Gallic and cries out to be filmed as a sentimental comedy'
Sunday Times

'At once tender and harrowing, light-hearted and profound, it is a highly original and affecting read' *The Lady*

'It's a powerful message which begins with the novel's title – a meditation on our obsession with beauty, celebrity and the consequences for those lumbered with one or both, delivered in a deceptively simple package stuffed full of filmic references and peppered with poetic quotations. It's a little gem and it's been a long time in the offing in translation' *A Life In Books*

Praise for *The List of My Desires*

'*The List of My Desires* is a gorgeous little novel . . . a fable-like tale of how money can't buy you happiness'
Stylist

'A runaway bestseller that looks set to follow the success of *The Elegance of the Hedgehog*. But that's not surprising – Grégoire Delacourt is an author who knows how to make his readers feel happy . . . [he]

describes the dilemmas of the heart and the vagaries of fate with tenderness and empathy' *Elle*

'A massive seller across Europe, this little book of Gallic charm is likely to warm British hearts too' *Choice*

'This thought-provoking debut from Grégoire Delacourt is a huge bestseller in France'

Good Housekeeping

'*The List of My Desires* has a natural charm and a clear sense of accomplishment' *L'Express*

'Impeccably translated from French by Anthea Bell, it's a sparkling and intriguing read . . . This is a very elegant novel. Its restraint is wonderful, with not a superfluous word. Grégoire Delacourt's keen eye pans deftly across the inner landscape of desire and longing, presenting a tender homage to almost unfashionable virtues – loyalty, duty, patience – without ever taking the high moral ground . . . These days, it is regarded as clichéd and hyperbolic to describe a novel as a tour de force. But I can't think of a more appropriate description for this book' *Irish Independent*

Grégoire Delacourt is the bestselling author of five novels and has won several literary awards. *The List of My Desires* was a runaway number-one bestseller in France, with rights sold in twenty-seven countries, and was selected for the Waterstones Book Club in the UK. *On ne voyait que le bonheur*, available from W&N as *We Only Saw Happiness* from late 2016, was short-listed for the Prix Goncourt 2014. Grégoire lives in Paris, where he runs an advertising agency with his wife.

www.gregoire-delacourt.com

Also available from W&N

The List of My Desires

the first *thing you* see

Grégoire Delacourt

Translated from the French by Anthea Bell

A W&N paperback

First published in Great Britain in 2015
by Weidenfeld & Nicolson

This paperback edition published in 2016
by Weidenfeld & Nicolson
an imprint of the Orion Publishing Group Ltd
Carmelite House, 50 Victoria Embankment
London EC4Y 0DZ
An Hachette UK Company

1 3 5 7 9 10 8 6 4 2

First published in France in 2013
as *La première chose qu'on regarde*
by Editions Jean-Claude Lattès

This book is supported by the Institut français (Royaume-Uni) as part of the Burgess programme.

A CIP catalogue record for this book is available from the British Library.

978 1 780 22664 4 (mass market paperback)

Printed in Great Britain by Clays Ltd, St Ives plc

www.orionbooks.co.uk

For Faustine, Blanche,
Grâce and Maximilien.

Arthur Dreyfuss liked big breasts.

He had wondered whether, if he had happened to be a girl, and because his mother's breasts were small but his grandmother's sizeable, at least in his memory of her suffocating hugs, his own would have been large or small.

He thought that a substantial chest made a woman walk in a more graceful, feminine way, and it was the grace of those delicately balanced figures that enchanted and sometimes deeply moved him. Ava Gardner in *The Barefoot Contessa*, Jessica Rabbit in *Who Framed Roger Rabbit?* And so many others. These images enraptured him, made him blush. A fine bosom was impressive; it made you fall silent, it called for respect. There wasn't a man on earth who didn't revert to being a little boy.

A man could die for such a thing.

Arthur Dreyfuss, who had never yet literally laid hands on them, had studied many different versions in back issues of *L'Homme moderne*, a magazine that he had discovered stashed away at his boss, PP's house. He had also seen them on the internet.

As for the real thing, there were Madame Rigaut-malolepszy's, spilling out of her blouse in spring: two gleaming watermelons so translucent that you could imagine pale green arteries bubbling just beneath the surface, tumultuous when she quickened her pace to catch the bus that stopped twice a day in the Grande Rue (really a small street into which a Scotsman by the name of Haywood had parachuted on 1 September 1944 to liberate the village) or when her nasty little russet-coloured dog, in a state of high excitement, dragged her off to investigate a pile of dog shit.

When young Arthur Dreyfuss reached year ten at school, his liking for such fleshy fruits induced him to sit near a girl called Nadège Lepetit who, oblivious to him as she was, wore a bra with a voluptuous size 38C cup, and thus had the advantage over the lovely Joëlle Ringuet, whose chest was as flat as a board. It was a bad choice. The unappreciative Nadège jealously protected her budding melons and wouldn't let greedy admirers near them. Aged thirteen and aware of her charms, Nadège wanted to be sure that she was loved for herself, and at that age Arthur Dreyfuss was not much good at fine words and deceptive verses. He hadn't read Rimbaud, and didn't really remember the sweet words of the songs of Cabrel, or the older songs of C. Jérôme (for instance, *Oh, do not leave me / Give yourself freely*).

When he discovered that Alain Roger, his friend at the time, had had the modest fruits of the ravishing Joëlle Ringuet at his fingertips, and then close to his lips, and then right inside his mouth, Arthur Dreyfuss thought he would go out of his mind and wondered whether he should revise his ideals and lower his expectations.

At the age of seventeen he went to Albert (the third largest town on the Somme) with the proud Alain Roger to celebrate his first payday. He chose to lose his virginity and experience vertiginous bliss with a well-endowed streetwalker, but was so impatient that he immediately paid tribute to his trousers instead. At this point he fled, ruined and ashamed, before he'd even had the chance to caress, feel, and embrace the girl's opalescent treasures.

This misfortune calmed his ardour. It put things in their proper place. He read two romantic novels by the American writer Karen Dennis, from which he learned that desire for another person is sometimes conveyed by a smile, a scent, or perhaps merely a look, as he discovered for himself six months later at Dédé's chip shop in the village – Dédé's was also a bar and tobacconist's that sold fishing gear, lottery tickets and newspapers as well. The fishermen were mainly interested in the bar. Its red Jupiler beer sign was their guiding star, shepherding them back home on interminable, freezing winter nights. It also attracted smokers, because no one took any notice of the 2006 anti-smoking law there.

That day, at Dédé's chip shop, something very simple happened to Arthur Dreyfuss: when asked what he would like, he raised his eyes and met the rainy grey eyes of the new waitress. They bowled him over. He also liked the sound of her voice, her smile, her pink gums, her white teeth, her perfume – all the beautiful things described by Karen Dennis. He forgot to look at her breasts, and for the first time he didn't mind whether they were discreetly small or appetisingly lavish. A flat plain or a hilly landscape, who cared?

It was a revelation: his first experience of love at first sight. And his first ventricular spasm – a kind of irregular heartbeat.

But nothing happened between him and the aforementioned waitress, because it would be no use beginning a love story at the end, especially as the waitress with the rainy grey eyes already had a lover, a truck driver who worked the Belgian and Dutch roads, a hefty guy with small but crushingly powerful hands and impressive biceps on which the name of his beloved was tattooed, Éloïse. She was taken, and by someone with a possessive streak. Everything Arthur Dreyfuss knew about karate and other martial arts he had learned from the blind master in *Kung Fu Panda* – the unforgettable Master Po – and from the savage cry of Pierre Richard in *The Return of the Tall Blond Man with One Black Shoe*, directed by Yves Robert. So he thought it best to forget the poetry of Éloïse's face, the rainy grey of her eyes, her pink gums; he stopped going to Dédé's for his morning coffee and even gave up smoking for fear of meeting the jealous truck driver.

To sum up this first chapter, it was on account of a sturdy and suspicious truck driver, on account of life in the little village of Long – population 687 persons, known as Longinians, situated on the Somme with its eighteenth-century château, its church steeple, its midsummer bonfires, its Cavaillé-Coll organ and its marshes, maintained in ecological balance by a few horses imported from the Camargue – and also on account of his profession as a motor mechanic, which leaves the fingers black and greasy, that at the age of twenty Arthur Dreyfuss, although an attractive young man (Éloïse had said he was like Ryan Gosling, only better-looking) lived alone in a small, isolated house on the way out of the village, set back from the D32 leading to Ailly-le-Haut-Clocher.

For anyone unacquainted with Ryan Gosling, he is a Canadian actor born on 12 November 1980 and he achieved worldwide success in 2011, a year after the date of the present story, with the magnificent and very dark film *Drive*, directed by Nicolas Winding Refn.

But never mind that.

On the day when this story begins, there was a knock on the door of Arthur Dreyfuss's house.

He was watching an episode of *The Sopranos* (season 3, episode 7: 'Uncle Junior has an operation for stomach cancer'). He jumped up. Cried out, 'Who's there?' The person knocked again. So he went to open the door. And he couldn't believe his eyes.

There, standing in front of him, was Scarlett Johansson.

Apart from getting horribly drunk at the third wedding of his boss Pascal Payen, known locally as PP – a drinking bout, incidentally, that left Arthur in such a stupor that he spent two days sucking on a watermelon – Arthur Dreyfuss didn't drink. Or only had a Kronenbourg in the evening now and then, in front of the TV.

So the hallucinatory vision of Scarlett Johansson standing on his front doorstep could not be put down to the ill effects of alcohol.

By no means.

Until that day, Arthur Dreyfuss had led a normal life. To give you a quick summary, and before we return to the disconcerting appearance of the actress, he was born in 1990 (the year of publication of the novel

Jurassic Park and of Tom Cruise's second marriage to Nicole Kidman) in the Camille-Desmoulins Maternity Hospital in Amiens, capital and administrative headquarters of the Picardy region, the son of Louis-Ferdinand Dreyfuss and Thérèse Marie Françoise Lecardonnel Dreyfuss.

An only child until 1994, when Noiya Dreyfuss arrived. Noiya means Beauty of God.

And he became an only child again in 1996, when Inke, the neighbour's powerful Dobermann, confused the Beauty of God with its dog food. The little girl's face and right hand emerged from Inke's other end as the waste product of *Canis lupus familiaris*, left behind in the shade of the wheel of a Grand Scenic. The local community supported the bereaved family as best it could. Little Arthur Dreyfuss shed no tears because they made his mother cry as well, reminding her of the horrors of this world, the supposed beauty of things, and God's shocking cruelty. And so the boy, an only child again, kept his grief to himself, like marbles concealed in the bottom of a pocket: little bits of glass.

People felt sorry for him, they ruffled his hair, they whispered, *poor boy* or *it's hard for a child*. This time in his life was both sad and happy. In the Dreyfuss family they ate a lot of stuffed dates, baklava and babaganoush, and in homage to the part of the family that came from

Picardy they indulged in cakes made with Maroilles cheese, and charlotte puddings flavoured with coffee and chicory. Sugar is fattening and it melts your sorrows away.

The bereaved family moved to the little town of Saint-Saëns in the Seine-Maritime department, on the outskirts of the state-owned forest of Eawy (pronounced *ay-ah-vee*), where Louis-Ferdinand Dreyfuss became a forestry worker. On certain evenings he returned home bearing pheasants, partridges, hares and other game, which his wife from Picardy made into pâtés, supremes and stews. Once he brought home the skin of a fox to be turned into a fur muff (winter was approaching), but Thérèse turned pale and cried out that she could never, never plunge her hands into a dead body.

One morning the poacher set out, as he did every morning, with his pouch and several traps over his shoulder. At the doorway, he said, also as he did every morning, *See you this evening!* But no one did see him that evening, or any other evening. The police were informed, but gave up looking for him a dozen days later. Madame, are you quite sure he doesn't have a little friend in town, a young girl, maybe? A man often goes missing for such reasons; it's a kind of an itch, he just wants to enjoy himself, he needs to feel alive, we've seen it all before. Not one trace of him, no footprints or fingerprints, no body. Thérèse Lecardonnel Dreyfuss quickly lost what little interest she still took in life and instead sought refuge in the Martini bottle each evening, at the time when the forestry worker used to come home, then earlier and earlier, until she started on the booze at the time he used to leave in the morning. At first, the vermouth (18 per cent) made her witty (Arthur Dreyfuss sometimes feels a certain quiet nostalgia for that), but then, little by little, it made her increasingly depressed and inclined, as in *The Open Window*, to see the ghost of the forestry worker reappearing at inappropriate moments. And then other ghosts.

A carnivorous quadruped.

An American actress who played Cleopatra.

Meat surrounding forearms.

Eyelids falling to dust.

In the evenings, Arthur Dreyfuss sometimes cried in his room when he heard Édith Piaf's sad, hoarse voice in the kitchen, and guessed at his mother's grief. He dared not say anything to her because he was afraid of losing her as well and finding himself alone. He didn't know how to tell her that he loved her; it seemed so difficult to say.

At school, Arthur Dreyfuss was an average pupil. Easy-going. Unbeatable at the game of jacks, which came back into fashion for a while. The girls liked him and voted him the second cutest boy in the class; the cutest of all was tall and darkly handsome, something of a Goth with his translucent complexion, the piercings here and there in his ears, as if showing you where to join up the dots, and the tattooed necklace round his throat (it depicted a twisted rope and was done after an alcohol-fuelled session reading Villon's *Ballade of the Hanged Men*). Above all, he was a poet, spouting far-fetched rhymes, murky consonances, silly sayings. For example: Life means nothing but decay; death lets you laugh another day. The girls loved him.

Arthur Dreyfuss's sole weakness was in PE. One day in the gym, watching a girl called Liane Le Goff jump the horse (she took a 36 DD, a cup size that could compete with Jayne Mansfield and Christina Hendricks), he fainted clean away.

His forehead hit the horse's metal foot, his skin cracked open and a drop of blood spurted out. His forehead was elegantly stitched and ever since he has had a discreet memento of that wonderful dizzy spell just under his eyebrow.

He doesn't dislike reading, far from it, and he loves watching films and television programmes – especially series, because then you have the time to get hooked, and to grow fond of the characters, like a little family.

He also enjoys taking anything with an engine or a mechanism apart and putting it back together again. People often asked him to decipher assembly instructions. The school found him a work experience position with Pascal Payen, known as PP, who represents several makes of car at his garage in Long, where one day Arthur Dreyfuss would obtain both a book of poetry and a fascinating job that would leave his fingers greasy and black.

He would tell ladies whose cars had broken down that he'd get them back on the road.

Darling, you're a genius, and good-looking too!

He would tell gentlemen whose cars had broken down that he'd get them back on the road.

Get a move on, then, boy, I have other things to do.

The job soon earned him enough to get a mortgage on a little house (two storeys, 67 square metres) on the outskirts of the village, set back from the D32 road leading to Ailly-le-Haut-Clocher, where, when there is a strong wind blowing, the countryside is full of the aroma of warm croissants and brioches topped with brown sugar coming from the Leguiff bakery. But there won't be any wind on the dramatic morning to which we shall come – and the day on which Scarlett Johansson will knock at the door of his little house.

So here she is again, at last.

Scarlett Johansson looked exhausted.

Her hair, somewhere in between two colours, was at war with itself, tumbling loose, flowing, as if in slow motion. Her luscious mouth had lost its usual gloss. There were gloomy shadows beneath her eyes where her mascara had smudged, like charcoal. And unfortunately for Arthur Dreyfuss, she was wearing a baggy sweater. A sweater like a sack that did no justice to the actress's curves, which everyone knew were bewitching, spellbinding.

She was holding a Vuitton bag in acid colours that made it look like a fake.

As for Arthur Dreyfuss, he was wearing what he usually wore to watch TV: a white undershirt and a pair of boxer shorts sporting a picture of the Smurfs. A long way from the image of Ryan-Gosling-only-better-looking.

All the same, as soon as they set eyes on each other they smiled.

Did they find one another handsome? Or reassuring? Perhaps, when there was such an urgent knocking on his door, Arthur had expected trouble with a cylinder head gasket, or a big end going, problems with a flow meter? When he opened the door, had she been expecting a pervert, a witch covered with warts, an old lady with a sweet little face? Whatever the case, it is a fact that the unlikely couple smiled as if pleasantly surprised, and Arthur Dreyfuss, who had just fallen in love at first sight for the second time in his life and was suffering the side effects (sweaty hands, rapid heartbeat, beads of perspiration, glacial little scalpels digging into his back, a frozen tongue) opened his dry mouth and uttered a word that does not exist.

Comine.

(For enquiring readers who take an interest in linguistics, and for amateur geographers, we may as well point out that there is, in fact, a town called Comines in the canton of Quesnoy-sur-Deûle in northern France, near the Belgian border – probably a rather sleepy little place, since there are at least five committees in the town trying to organise festivals to shake it up – but that has nothing to do with the present story.)

The moment Arthur Dreyfuss saw Scarlett Johansson standing in his doorway, his timid *Comine* instinctively struck him as the most appropriate, most courteous, and in general the best thing to say, because, according to the subtitles for the TV series that he was watching in the original version, those words were the English equivalent of '*Entrez*'.

And what man in the world, even one wearing an undershirt and boxer shorts with Smurfs on them, would not have said '*Comine*' to the amazing star of *Lost in Translation*?

The amazing star whispered, '*Thank you*', in English, the pink tip of her tongue showing between her lips as she pronounced the *th*, and came in.

As he quietly closed the door, hands sweating and heart suddenly switching up into an even higher gear – yes, he was going to die, and yes, he *could* die happy now – Arthur glanced furtively round to see if there were cameras outside, and/or bodyguards, and/or some professional practical joker from a TV station. Then, still not entirely reassured, he bolted the door.

Two years earlier, the police had brought a car into PP's garage, the wreck of a Peugeot 406 that had just somersaulted five times on the D112 near Cocquerel (2.42 kilometres away from Long as the crow flies).

It was night.

The driver had been going fast; he seemed to have lost control of the car, skidding on the treacherous layer of water that oozed like translucent algae from the uneven surface of the country road where it passed the Étangs des Provisions. The two occupants had died instantly. The firemen had had to cut off the man's legs to get him out of the car. The passenger's face had been crushed against the windscreen and a lock of her blonde hair was caught in the star-shaped patch of glass, together with a lozenge of blood. When, on PP's instructions, he had examined the interior of the wreck, Arthur Dreyfuss had found a book of poetry on the passenger seat and instantly, as if by a reflex action, tucked it into one of the large pockets of his dungarees. What was a poetry book doing in a car where two people had just died? Had the passenger been reading the driver a poem when the car came off the road? Who were they? Were they leaving each other, or meeting each other again? Had they decided to put an end to it all together?

That evening, alone in his little house, Arthur had opened the book, his fingers trembling slightly. The collection was entitled *Existing*, and the author's name was Jean Follain. There was a lot of white on each page, and in the middle of it short lines, little furrows carved out by the ploughshare of letters. He read simple words that seemed to describe very profound things, like these, which evoked for him his father:

> *. . . and beneath his strong arm*
> *Not even looking at the trees*
> *he doggedly held*
> *all the figures of the world.* *

* Jean Follain, 'Atlas', *Territoires* (Gallimard, 1953).

And these, which might have been about Noiya and their mother:

. . . and here is she who will die young
*and she whose body alone is left.**

There wasn't a word that he failed to understand, but the way they were put together astonished him. He had a confused feeling that words he knew, if ornamented with pearls in a certain way, could change his perception of the world. Could celebrate the grace of ordinary things, for instance – ennobling the simple.

Over the next few months he relished the other wonderful arrangements of words in the book. To him, they seemed like a gift that might help tame the extraordinary, if ever it should come knocking at the door.

For instance on Wednesday, 15 September 2010, at 7.47 in the evening, when the stunning Scarlett Johansson, American actress born on 22 November 1984 in New York, was suddenly standing in front of you, Arthur Dreyfuss, French motor mechanic, an astounded Longinian, born in 1990.

How could it be possible?

* Jean Follain, 'Les Enfants', *Territoires* (Gallimard, 1953).

Why did no poetic words spring to his lips? Why did his dreams paralyse him when they actually came true? Why was the first thing that Arthur Dreyfuss managed to ask whether she spoke French? Because, as far as I'm concerned, he added slowly in French, blushing, English might as well be double Dutch.

Scarlett Johansson raised her head with a graceful movement and told him, with almost no accent, or only a very subtle and delicious one, sweet as a Ladurée macaroon, an accent that was a cross between Romy Schneider's and Jane Birkin's: yes, I speak French, and so does my friend Jodie. Jodie Foster! exclaimed Arthur, impressed, you know Jodie Foster? Then he shrugged his shoulders and murmured, as if to himself: of course, of course, how stupid of me. Because it is a fact that at the start of an encounter of this kind, intelligence seldom gets the better of stupefaction.

However, women have a gift for helping men out of their difficulties, of rescuing them when they flounder, and reassuring them.

Scarlett Johansson smiled at him and then, with a warm sigh, took off her baggy sweater, hand-knitted in clamshell stitch, with the elegance of Grace Kelly in *Rear Window* taking her muslin nightdress out of a tiny handbag. It's lovely in your house, the actress murmured. The mechanic's heart was racing again. He was very lightly clad, but suddenly he felt hot. He closed his eyes for an instant as if he were in the midst of a dizzy spell, something both sweet and terrifying – his mother dancing naked in the kitchen. When he opened his eyes again, the New York star was wearing a bustier, pearly white and silky, with lace shoulder straps. It fitted her breasts like a glove (he crossed his legs to quell the start of an erection), but also, and this moved and almost shocked the motor mechanic, it revealed a sensuous little roll of fat near her navel, a suntanned little ring like a chubby doughnut. It's lovely in your house, the actress murmured. Yes . . . yes, stammered Arthur Dreyfuss, suddenly regretting the absence of good lines of dialogue in real life: a virile monologue such as a screenwriter like Michel Audiard might have supplied, some cogent responses from the pen of a Henri Jeanson.

They looked at each other again: he a little pale with scarlet blotches on his face, she with a wonderfully pink complexion, a perfect little Barbie doll. They coughed at the same time, and at the same time each began to speak. You first, he said. No, no, please, you first, she replied. He coughed a little more, to gain time, to enable him to assemble words and then join them up in a pretty phrase, like that poet. But the soul of the mechanic came out on top. You . . . did you break down? he asked.

Scarlett Johansson burst out laughing. She has such a lovely laugh, he thought, and oh, those white teeth.

No, I didn't break down.

Because I work in a garage and . . . and I get people up and running again.

I didn't know, she said in English.

I mean, the cars, it's the cars I get up and running . . .

I don't have a car, she said, not here. I came by coach. Back in Los Angeles I have a hybrid, everyone does, but a hybrid never breaks down because it doesn't really have an engine.

Then the son of a silent father, the father who had disappeared, called on all his courage as a man in the making, stood up, and said in a voice that hardly trembled at all:

What are you doing here, Scarlett? Sorry. I mean, Madame.

A brief reminder.

The star awarded the distinction of having 'the best breasts in Hollywood' by the *Access Hollywood* television show (for curious readers, and others who have an interest in the subject, Salma Hayek came second, Halle Berry third, Jessica Simpson fourth and Jennifer Love Hewitt fifth), had had a love affair and practised tantric sex with the actor Josh Hartnett from 2004 to 2006.

Then, in 2007, she met Ryan Reynolds in a New York cinema.

It was the beginning of an idyll.

For her new lover's thirty-first birthday, Scarlett Johansson (then twenty-three years old) gave him one of her wisdom teeth that had been extracted, first getting it dipped in gold so that he could wear it on a chain round his neck – more chic and very much trendier than a shark's tooth. Let those who think that such a present might undermine the elegance of new love admit their error: in May 2008, the two turtledoves got engaged. But hadn't the voluptuous star said, in January 2008, that she wasn't ready to get married? 'I'm not ready for the Big Day.' Anyway, in September 2008, Ryan Reynolds, a Canadian, married his American fiancée in Vancouver. The couple were love's sweet dream, and if love really does only last three years, as one successful book claimed, then it was beating its wings ready to go long before that time was up.

I couldn't take it any longer, Scarlett Johansson continued, while Arthur Dreyfuss, after making her two cups of Ricoré instant coffee, had gone on himself to Kronenbourg lager. I just couldn't take it, she repeated, I needed some fresh air, so I came here without my husband for the Deauville Festival.

But Deauville is 180 kilometres away, said Arthur Dreyfuss, baffled.

I know, but when I got to Deauville I felt scared, she admitted, her voice suddenly lower. I didn't want to find myself in the spotlight again (she spoke the word *spotlight* as if she were sucking a sweet, with a little bubble of saliva breaking on her lips), especially as I don't have a movie competing in the American Film Festival this year. So I got on a coach; I wanted to go to Le Touquet and stay in a little hotel, incognito, and here I am.

What do you mean?

I mean, well, I'm here.

But this isn't Le Touquet. It's Long, and there are ponds here, and water bugs that dance across the water at night, and the noise of animals, and owls hooting, but there's definitely no sea.

You're so cute.

Scarlett Johansson had thought of going to the 36th American Film Festival at Deauville that year, but had changed her mind at the last moment.

Like many unhappy people who want to go missing so that someone will find them.

We all know stories of veins being unsuccessfully cut and overdoses that were miscalculated. They are always cries for help, calling out. Then finally a faint little voice, lost, that no one understands.

Arthur Dreyfuss, a splendid sight in his undershirt and his Smurfs boxer shorts, opened another Kronenbourg, offered it to her this time, and asked his question again. *What are you doing here, Scarlett?*

I want to disappear for a few days.

The statement moved Arthur Dreyfuss deeply.

He made his decision within two seconds. He would help, protect, hide and rescue the unhappy actress. He would take care of the incognito star. The magnificent runaway. He would be a hero, like the good guys in films, steadfast and ready for anything, the kind of man on whose shoulder inaccessible beauties would shed their tears, confess their tragic fate, and in the end, after many twists and turns of the plot, fall in love with him.

Too bad if it transformed his life.

So he offered his bed to 'the best breasts in Hollywood', saying he would be fine on the sofa.

He showed her round his house, which was tiny, so it didn't take long. Here, on the ground floor, was the living room and the kitchen. A three-seater Ektorp sofa from Ikea. It cost only 40 euros more than the two-seater, he explained. It was a fine day when I got it, so I put it together outside and my boss, PP, lent a hand. But when it was assembled, with the armrests and all, we couldn't get it back inside, so PP, mad with rage, took the front door off its hinges and in the end we managed to push it through, but the upholstery fabric at the back got torn. Luckily it doesn't show too much. There was also a well-worn wicker armchair, a table, and a great deal of chaos – dirty dishes and so on.

I wasn't expecting you today, he apologised, laughing. She blushed. The bathroom was on the first floor, pale blue tiles – blue for a boy – with a large cast-iron bathtub like a mini ocean-going liner on the tiled sea. Let's pass over the toilet, all the underpants and socks – hey presto, tidied away!

Here are two clean towels, I've got more if you need them, and here's a wash mitt that's never been used, but . . . er, that doesn't mean that I don't . . .

She smiled, an irresistible, understanding smile.

. . . and shampoo, and a new bar of sweet almond soap; look, it says so on the label.

On the second floor, his bachelor bedroom, night falling outside the small window, the moon, the imaginary forms you think you can see in the natural world. On the walls: posters of Michael Schumacher, Ayrton

Senna, Denise Richards, a naked Megan Fox, Whitney Houston; section drawings of the V10 engine of a Dodge Viper and of a flat-6 Porsche engine.

Don't you have a photograph of me? she asked a little mischievously, as he changed the sheets. He blushed.

She helped him to make the bed tidy, a situation that troubled him for a moment because there isn't a man in the world who wouldn't dream of making his bed *untidy* with the assistance of Scarlett Johansson.

I know what you're thinking, she whispered, and it's touching. Thank you.

He smiled at her timidly, because he didn't know what to make of that whisper.

Before leaving to go back to his three-seater Ektorp sofa, Arthur asked her what she would like for breakfast (an American coffee and a French croissant, please), and then they wished each other good night in the most natural way imaginable (*Bonne nuit*, he said in French; *Good night*, she said in English), and this unexpected intimacy, if it made her happy for a moment, grieved him because of everything he felt that he had lost in the chaos of his childhood.

Such comfortable affection, with no ulterior motives.

Of course, Arthur Dreyfuss didn't sleep very well that night. What do you expect?

Suppose you'd heard water running in the bathroom. Imagined water being scooped up in the palm of her hand, her hand running down over her neck, her throat, water trickling down her skin, the gooseflesh rising as her skin reacted to the cold. Now Scarlett Johansson is two floors above you, in your bed, in your sheets, maybe naked, and there's nothing between the two of you but the thirty-nine steps of the staircase. There isn't even a bolt on your bedroom door. There are no neighbours living nearby. No one would hear anyone crying out. Nor is there the sound of a helicopter, there are no dazzling pursuits, no monstrous black 4x4s like shadows, the sort you see in American films; there's no indication of a hunt for the runaway celebrity, nothing suggesting that this is all some big joke. It's all real. Terribly real.

There's only silence.

The silence of the night that frightens the villagers, because the ponds are so close by, moving shadows, the moon shedding light on the lies human beings tell, because of legends, the legend of a poacher who disappeared, of an animal, maybe, one of those described by Follain: *All the creatures of its species / live on in it.**

There's only silence.

* Jean Follain, 'La Bête', *Exister* (Gallimard, 1947).

And your desire.

Your fear. Your damp fingers. Your incomprehension, too, surfacing with a touch of unease, your unexpected anger with this crazy situation: what's she doing here anyway? It's impossible, downright impossible. Common sense insinuates itself, struggling, making its way into all the brutality and chaos; you cling to any explanation, it doesn't matter what: it's something for television, it can't be anything else, a new comic turn by François Damiens, a new programme from TV host Ruquier, maybe the return of producer Dominique Cantien. You feel the dull threat of madness. This kind of dream doesn't exist, a star turning into reality, into flesh and blood. You know it can't be right: Scarlett Johansson ringing your doorbell, smiling at you and sleeping beneath your sheets. There has to be some explanation. Like the conjurors who cut the legs off pretty women, who saw off heads, resuscitate doves that they've dismembered, laughing all the while.

The hours pass by. And you decide to . . . but your cowardice comes out on top, no man likes to fall flat on his face. And then doubt comes into it, too (suppose, just suppose she didn't say no?) In the end you go upstairs quietly, on tiptoe. You take care not to tread on the seventh, thirteenth, fifteenth, twenty-second and twenty-third steps because they creak, you also avoid the eighth because it squeals like a mouse caught in a trap, and you don't want to run the risk of being thought a thug. But suddenly your fears die down. You hear her breathing, you hear a soft, very soft snore, like the purring of a cat that has just stuffed itself with the above-mentioned mouse. And you are moved by her weakness. Her fragility. And for a moment Scarlett Johansson, the girl in your bed, is no longer the world-famous sex bomb but simply a sleeping girl.

Only a sleeping girl. Only *this* beautiful sleeping girl.

Arthur Dreyfuss went downstairs again slowly, like a sleepwalker, avoiding the giveaway steps, and collapsed on the sofa.

What would you do in my position, Papa? What would you do? Speak to me, tell me, where are you? Do you sometimes come to see me at night, do you still think of me?

Have you left us, or are you lost?

In PP's garage next morning, Arthur had to drain and check the levels of fluid in a Clio, change the segments of a piston in a 205 GTI dating from 1986 (a genuine antique), and check the wheel alignment of a Toyota Starlet. Starlet: the name made him smile.

A garage like any other village garage. A big wooden gate with the words *Payen Service Station* painted on it in large, washed-out lettering. Inside, a mechanised inspection pit, dozens of punctured tyres, shiny cans of oil, dirt, greasy tools, dusty fingerprints, and everywhere on the walls packs of Varta batteries; some enamelled plaques – Veedol, Olazur, Essolube, and an obsolete pump for Solexine autolubricating fuel. Under a tarpaulin at the back there was a 1965 Aronde 1300 Weekend that PP had promised himself he was going to restore some day, rust corroding it a little more with each day that passed.

Just as it corrodes the souls of those who never realise their dreams.

Mid-morning Arthur Dreyfuss took advantage of a little test drive of the Starlet to go past his house incognito and see if Scarlett Johansson was still there. If he'd been dreaming. If there were journalists surrounding the house. A horde of them. When he saw that stunning silhouette walking back and forth at his kitchen window, and not a soul outside the house, his heart swelled (it went *Boom*, like the Charles Trenet song: *Boom, when our hearts go* boom, *Everything else says* boom) and he was happy.

About one o'clock, after eating a sandwich sent for him from Dédé's bar and tobacconist's which also sold fishing articles, newspapers and lottery tickets, where he himself couldn't set foot any more because of the rain-coloured eyes of Éloïse and the glowering menace of the long-distance truck driver, Arthur Dreyfuss asked PP if he could use the office computer.

I need to do some research into a compression wheel for a turbo, he told his boss.

He typed 'Scarlett Johansson' into Google.

On 6 September she had been at a publicity photo shoot for Mango, a fashion chain, in the United States.

On 8 September she had been spotted boarding a plane at Los Angeles airport.

On the 14th she was seen in Roissy wearing dark glasses, a hat and black leggings, with a grey shawl. On the same day she had been in Épernay, at the Tribute to Heritage evening organised by Moët et Chandon, wearing a Vuitton dress, and she had been photographed with, among others, Arjun Rampal (a handsome Indian actor, star of *Hunko Tumse Pyaar Hai* and *Om Shanti Om*).

Then nothing.

On the evening of 15 September, she had knocked on Arthur Dreyfuss's door, but the internet didn't mention that.

Then he typed 'Deauville, Festival. American film'.

The festival had ended three days earlier, on 12 September, and Émanuelle Béart, presiding over the jury, had awarded the prize (to Rodrigo Garcia's *Mother and Child*, the story of a girl, Karin, who got pregnant at fourteen) and then invited everyone to attend the following year. When the garage mechanic had closed the Google home page, before returning to his compression wheel and other crankcase decompression devices, he was faced with two questions.

Why had Scarlett Johansson lied about Deauville?

How had her hair grown a good ten centimetres in one day?

When he got home that evening, perhaps because he had worked out answers to his two earlier questions, Arthur was rather nervous. Scarlett Johansson was still there; she had tidied up the little house, she had probably watched TV. A whole day doing nothing is a long time (particularly in the village of Long).

She had made pasta with cheese sauce.

It's comfort food, she said. It's what you eat in America, with the family, when you want to feel good, when it's cold or when you're feeling a little depressed. Food that makes you feel comfortable, like you had in your childhood. Like a warm blanket, or the arms of someone you miss.

Arthur Dreyfuss wondered whether she missed her own childhood. He thought, of course, of his little sister Noiya, who had never even had the chance to learn how to say his first name properly. He thought of his mother, who used to dance listening to Édith Piaf; he thought of the vermouth waving about furiously as she held it in the air. He thought of his lost father, who had flown away, might be perching somewhere, no doubt on the branch of a wild cherry tree. He thought that his childhood had been so short, so empty and sad that maybe he didn't really miss it – an amputation far back in the past . . . it was only now and then, in the cold morning hours by the ponds of La Catiche or Dix, with his father's silence, his reassuring masculine odour, that the amputated part of him itched.

Although he was beginning to get his head round the surreal idea that Scarlett Johansson might indeed have run away and landed in his house (but how and why?), he found it extremely disconcerting (and also extremely exciting) to be welcomed home by the star – nominated four times for the Golden Globes, winner of the People's Choice Award in 2007 and of two Chlotrudis Awards, the title of Woman of the Year 2007 awarded by Hasty Pudding Theatricals, also a winner at the Venice Film Festival in 2003, the Gotham Awards 2008, etc. – with a tea towel patterned with Portobello mushrooms tied round her waist, and about to put the cheese pasta into the oven.

Is something wrong? she asked, with her sensuous mouth. Aren't you hungry?

Y . . . yes, stammered Arthur Dreyfuss. It's just that I feel as if I'm standing beside myself, outside my own body, in another life, I mean.

And you don't like it?

Yes. Yes, I do.

But it scares you?

A little, yes. It's unreal. And the oddest thing about it is that there isn't a hysterical crowd out there, no journalists, no fans, no crazies wanting to see you, touch you, fight to have their photo taken with you.

Because this is the backside of beyond, she said, delicately alluring.

He smiled. You mean the back of beyond?

Yes, and that's the best place to disappear. Who would ever think of looking for me here, Arthur?

It was a good argument. Arthur sat down on the arm of the Ektorp sofa.

That's exactly the reason I came here. To get away from everything. To get away from the pressure. To get away from Ryan. (She meant Ryan Reynolds, her husband.) To get away from my agent and my mom, Melanie. Tears came to her eyes. I just wanted a few days of normal life. Only a few days. I wanted to be a girl like any other for once in my life. An ordinary girl, almost boring. Like the girls who hand out the special deals for chicken in Wal-Mart. I wanted to be forgotten for a few days. Miss Nobody. Above all, not Scarlett Johansson. I'm sure you can understand that. I want to be able to go out without any make-up on, wearing the same T-shirt as the day before, with a Peruvian hat on my head, without being afraid I might find myself on the cover of some horrible magazine with a headline like *Scarlett Johansson plunges into depression*.

She mopped away the tears that were running down to her chin.

I just want to be quiet for a few days, Arthur. Just that. Be myself without the facade, the illusions. That's all. I'm not asking for the moon, am I? Just that.

At this point Arthur Dreyfuss, who didn't know much about tenderness, stood up, stepped forward and took her in his arms. He realised in that moment that she wasn't very tall, but her breasts were large, because they touched his torso at a reasonable and polite distance. The actress sobbed for a while. She said a few words in English, which Arthur Dreyfuss did not understand, except for *fed up*, which he thought he had heard before in a couple of television series, *24* and *The Wire*, and then he thought to himself that he really ought to be the one who was fed up because when an erotic dream steps into your life and knocks on your door, you might expect it to love you, kiss you, kill you – but not to dissolve in tears on your shoulder, the shoulder of a garage mechanic.

You expect a moment of light, and grace.

He thought of a little collection of words and smiled. One day he'd venture it. *Leaning on his lover's arm / bearing the weight of her beauty / hunted in the shelter of her corset.*[*]

They ate the pasta, and Scarlett Johansson livened up, her high cheekbones shining.

She talked about Woody Allen, 'the sexiest man on the planet', I've never laughed so much with anyone; about Penelope Cruz, she's my sister, my soulmate, I love her; about her sixth part in a film at the age of thirteen(!), as Grace MacLean in *The Horse Whisperer*, I adored Robert (Redford); about 'her girls', as she called her breasts, and how Natalie Portman was admiring of them. She laughed, and Arthur Dreyfuss thought she was beautiful when she laughed, even if he thought, without being able to draw up the full list yet, that there must be at least a thousand better things to do with Scarlett Johansson than just sit here eating pasta in cheese sauce. For instance, reading her some poems, caressing her earlobe, exterminating all Dobermann

* Jean Follain, 'Aux choses lentes', *Exister* (Gallimard, 1947).

and Rottweiler dogs, just to be on the safe side, thinking of names for children, tickling her little golden doughnut, choosing a desert island where the two of them could live, brushing her hair while listening to a Neil Young song, eating violet or liquorice-flavoured macaroons, etc.

She talked about her Danish grandfather, Ejner, a scriptwriter and director (*En maler og hans*) then her architect father, Karsten, and Arthur couldn't help thinking of his own father who had never come home.

She talked a lot and she ate a lot. You'd have thought she was catching up, getting her revenge on the 'Hollywood regime' (Judy Mazel's Beverly Hills Diet, which consisted mainly of fruit and vegetables), getting her own back on all those concerted efforts that made her one of the most glamorous women in the world at the age of twenty-seven. A blonde with over seventy million pages on Google. All the same, Arthur Dreyfuss (who wasn't used to drinking several Kronenbourgs in a row) thought her nose was a little long, her chin pointed, her lips slightly full, while her skin shone and her breasts were incredible.

Are you listening to me, Arthur?

Yes, yes, I am, he mumbled, putting down his fork. In fact, even with Éloïse of the rainy eyes at Dédé's chip shop, words had never come easily to him.

I, I . . . it's astounding to have you here, Scarlett, it's . . .

It's astounding for me, too, she interrupted, this is the first evening in a long while when I've been left in peace, when I could eat as much pasta as I wanted without someone saying, *Go easy on the pasta, Scarlett, you know how you tend to put on weight*, and it takes forever, simply forever, to lose it. This is the first evening when I can lick my fingers without someone saying don't do that, Scarlett, it's vulgar, a mouth, a finger, it's obscene; and all that in the company of a super, super cute guy who hasn't tried to jump on me right away, whose eyes aren't riveted to my boobs as if he were a halfwit – that's the right word, isn't it, Arthur, halfwit?

Arthur Dreyfuss blushed and felt slightly wounded, because last night, two floors down, he had indeed wanted to jump on her, and he'd been feeling the same way all morning at the garage. Even if she did have a long nose, a pointed chin, a soft little roll of fat, and that small black spot near her right ear that had just appeared like a flower bud – a tiny dark orchid that had bloomed a little earlier in the evening.

When he cleared the table, she thanked him, and he was overwhelmed. One of the most beautiful girls in the world was in his kitchen, thanking him: thanking him for the pasta, thanking him for the beer, thanking him for the not very interesting conversation.

He dared not say too much for fear of spoiling that beautiful moment.

He washed the dishes while she examined his neatly arranged DVDs: oh, I love boxed sets, too, she exclaimed, it's like having a family when you don't have one any more – you can have a little reunion every evening. *The Sopranos*, of course, I just love it; *24*, *The Wire, The Shield, The Great Escape, Matrix, La Dolce Vita* (not the Fellini version but the one made by someone called Mario Salieri, with Kasumi and Rita Faltoyano, by the spirited producer of erotic films, Marc Dorcel).

Oh, he cried, letting go of a plate which broke in the sink. That one's not mine, I, I must give it back . . . a mate of mine . . . a mate at the garage . . . Hands covered with foam, he tried to grab the offending article, but she wouldn't let go; suddenly they were like two kids playing, innocent, just messing about. Give it back! No, I won't! Give it back! Come and get it! Come on, come on – and they laughed and everything was suddenly so simple.

Arthur Dreyfuss hadn't said anything.

He wanted one more day with her – two days, eight days – like in the Édith Piaf song.

Listen, PP, what would you do if Angelina Jolie dropped by your house?

The face of PP (who looked rather like the actor Gene Hackman – a young Gene Hackman, at the time of *The French Connection* and *Scarecrow*) appeared, sliding out from under a Peugeot 605 and covered with smiles. Would my wife be at home?

Arthur Dreyfuss shrugged his shoulders. Stop it, PP, I'm being serious.

You went out last night, didn't you, Arthur? Had a drop too much to drink, laddie?

Another shrug of the shoulders.

Well, okay, I'd try to screw her. Wouldn't you?

Yes, sure.

Hey, is Angelina Jolie the star who was in *Tomb Raider*?

Yup.

I'd certainly mount a raid on her! Ha, ha, ha . . . a raid on her, get it? That's a good one!

Seriously, PP, wouldn't you wonder why she'd turned up at your place?

The rest of PP gracefully followed his head out from under the car. He got to his feet and his face, which was smeared with oil, turned serious. There's always a good reason for everything, kid. If your Angelina Jolie came to my place – and it's just as well that's not possible – it would be like a gift, because beauty is always a gift, especially with breasts and a mouth like that. It'd make you want to believe in angels and all that bullshit, because there could be only one reason why she'd come here.

What reason? asked Arthur Dreyfuss, his heart fluttering.

Love, my boy, love. Now then, could be she'd turn up here because she's been driving around these parts and her cylinder head gasket has just blown – and let me remind you that you're a garage mechanic – well, I'd repair her gasket straightaway, I'd ask for her autograph, maybe I'd even invite her to have a coffee at Dédé's chip shop so as to make believe, for just one moment, that she and I were a couple, so as to be seen with her, so people would say, 'Did you see the stunner

PP's taking out?', but . . . but sometimes it might not even be Angelina Jolie! Look, Léon, they'd say, PP's going out with that actress, she's hot, and she'd be recognised, and for a second or so I'd be like a god, yes, like a god, my boy, I'd be Angelina Jolie's guy. The man who held heaven in his arms.

A wave of sorrow surged over Arthur Dreyfuss, making him shiver.

He knew exactly what PP was talking about. The impossible dream. The myth of the beauty with a heart of gold, a woman coveted by every man on the planet but who suddenly chooses him, the goddess who gives up everyone else – three and a half billion others at the very least.

Grace Kelly had preferred Prince Rainier to Count Oleg Cassini, to Jack Kennedy (the fashion designer), to Bing Crosby, to Cary Grant, to Jean-Pierre Aumont, to Clark Gable, to Frank Sinatra, to Tony Curtis, to David Niven, to Ricardo Boccelli, to Anthony Havelock-Allan, to so many others. She made the easy-going Rainier someone different, a man like no one else in the world.

She made him into a god.

And when PP confessed, in a slightly husky voice: you know, Arthur, if I'd been born in the 1920s and I'd been Marilyn Monroe's guy, she'd never have made her life such a misery with all that stupid shit, I just know that she wouldn't. She didn't need footballers, actors, presidents, pretentious writers, men who loved themselves more than her. No, what her heart needed was a simple, honest fellow who liked other people, say a garage owner, a guy who could take her out for a drive to see pretty things, put down the hood so that she could breathe in the crisp air of autumn, so that she could taste the rain, tiny little drops full of dust, swollen by the wind – someone who'd hold her hand without squeezing it, without stifling her, without trying to screw her on the back seat. That's what I'd have done if Marilyn had been my girl, and that's why she'd have died of old age beside me, yup . . . when PP said all that, Arthur Dreyfuss felt like crying.

On the third evening of his life with Scarlett Johansson, Arthur Dreyfuss came home with *Vicky Cristina Barcelona* and *The Island*, the two DVDs that he had managed to find at the Planchard hairdressing salon (where you could also leave your ink and laser cartridges to be refilled). Easily recognisable by its boring brick facade, the salon had two little picture windows, a red brick mezzanine floor and a washed-out sign saying *Édonil Hair Care*. He was also carrying their dinner: cheese puff-pastry rolls (cheese again!), two plates of charcuterie, and a bottle of wine from Tonnelier – butcher, delicatessen and catering – in the Rue du 12 Novembre 1918.

The butcher's shop was a place that never dated. It was like something out of a Depardon photo, with its red and white facade and its black lettering, capitals with serious-looking serifs, like the lettering in a radiologist's consulting room, each letter stuck on a different white cube. If there hadn't been any cars or advertisements in the background you might have thought you were back in the 1950s. In Long, time seemed to have stood still, with its low-built houses, made of brick or cement, pitched tiled roofs, walls painted cheerful colours – yellow, ochre, or a happy sky-blue like the butcher's shop. The shop stood on the corner of Rue Hotton and Rue l'Ancienne-École-des-Filles, and no doubt the colour was an attempt to counter the dull, melancholy grey sky overhead, a grey militating against any flights of fancy.

It was Arthur Dreyfuss's turn to supply comfort food, by way of cushioning the blow that he was about to deliver.

Scarlett Johansson seemed much moved by his thoughtfulness and ventured to drop a playful kiss on the motor mechanic's cheek, which almost made him drop the plates of cold meat, a clumsiness that made him appeal even more to the young actress – or at least he thought so.

She suggested a little walk round the village before dinner. I've got pins and needles in my legs, she said, smiling. She looked charming and engaging. Arthur

Dreyfuss agreed enthusiastically. It was like the unexpected present of several extra minutes of life before a bad verdict.

He waited for the sun to move beyond the ponds of Les Provisions and Les Aunais, casting dense and comforting shadows, perfect cover for a star going for a walk incognito. Then they went out into the quiet village of Long, shivering in the muggy dampness of the marshes. It was a small village and it took them only about twenty minutes to walk past the château, the hydroelectric power station, the Grande Rue (containing the town hall, the Senior Citizens' Club, the bakery – pizza baked on Thursdays, *Remember to Tell Us Your Order*), the municipal campsite known as The Poplars, the Copin dairy farm and Gervais-Scombart the builder's.

They walked through the first of the smoke rising from chimneys, less than a metre apart, with him lagging a little way behind her, and sometimes, when their shadows were cast against a wall, he put out his shadow hand to caress her shadow hair. He trembled almost as much as if it had been a real caress; he was taming himself, trying out new gestures of affection; suddenly he felt he would have liked to talk, to tell her, in the kindly darkness, the words you assemble in your head at night, preparing for the next day when a moment like this comes along. Scarlett Johansson was looking around her; she was laughing, a simple, happy laugh. But words are cowardly and they conceal themselves; they shy away before the conjugation of a dream body, become confused when faced with the forthright grammar of desire; all words are useless in the raw presence of things.

Are you all right? she asked.

I . . . I. Yes. You're not cold?

They were passing the tiny chapel of Our Lady of Lourdes on the way out of the village, heading towards Ailly. He would have liked to be an impulsive man, strong and sturdy, vehement under the influence of his own desires; he would have liked to push her into the chapel, she would have let out a little cry (probably), she would have said, you're crazy, she would have asked, what are you doing? And he would have said, I'm going to ask you to share your life with me, to choose a desert island, to eat violet-flavoured macaroons, and she would have laughed and repeated *you're crazy*; she would have said, let's go back now, yes, I am a little cold, but that was nice of you, Arthur, really nice, it's cute.

She might have said yes.

But Arthur remained silent because a person's weaknesses always get the upper hand.

He remained silent because you can't win over the

impossible, a girl like Scarlett Johansson, with your impetuous urgency; you need elegance, a kind of renunciation.

Let's go back, he said. You're a little cold.

Yet he was the one trembling, because he knew what was going to happen next.

They set up their dinner in front of the TV and started by watching *The Island*. Arthur Dreyfuss liked action movies better than the romantic sort – which was how he imagined the films of an ageing Woody Allen would be, tainted by the slightly suspect feelings of a man who had left his wife to sleep with their adopted daughter. But anyway, we'll watch them both, he had said, and during the film Scarlett Johansson had talked a lot, sometimes even with her mouth full. Shc made comments on every scene: they filmed this bit in the Nevada desert; I just love Ewan (McGregor) in that white tracksuit, he's so sexy, so hot. Look at that, Lincoln's car (Lincoln was the character played by Ewan McGregor in the film), it's a Cadillac, it cost seven million dollars, think of that, seven million dollars because of all the special effects! She attacked a second puff-pastry roll. It was terribly difficult to shoot those scenes, she said. Did you know I had an operation just before the film was made? They took out my tonsils and every day the director, Michael Bay's office phoned to find out how I was doing. To check when I'd be able to go back to the gym, because it was a very physical role, simply exhausting, and everyone was in a panic and . . .

And here Arthur Dreyfuss joined in. And you had splints put on your tibias after the chase scenes.

The actress suddenly stopped eating her puff-pastry roll, her mouth stayed open, and all the blood seemed to drain from her face. For a second she almost looked ugly. And you had terrible trouble with your knee, I know. I read it on *Allociné*. I expect you did, too.

He took a little piece of paper out of his pocket and slowly, almost cruelly, unfolded it.

When you read the script you were delighted by the relationship between your character and Lincoln. You said: Those two don't know anything about intimacy and sexuality. They're totally naive, because they've lived in a kind of plastic bubble, isolated from the outside world. In its way it's a wonderful love story.

Scarlett Johansson put her hand to her mouth and

discreetly spat out her mouthful of Tonnelier's cheese roll. Her lips were pale and trembling.

My name is Jeanine Foucamprez, she said.

Jeanine

Arthur Dreyfuss was both disappointed and relieved.

His disappointment stemmed from the fact that, just like PP with Angelina Jolie, he had dreamed for a moment, just a split second, the space in time of a sigh, of being 'Scarlett Johansson's guy' – although PP never had been and never would be 'Angelina Jolie's guy' – and he had liked the idea. It had seemed to him that with the glamorous actress in his arms, like an angel, like a blessing, he would at last have been that elect someone among three and a half billion other men: the only man in the world capable of saving Marilyn Monroe from dying on 5 August 1962 by taking her out to enjoy the dusty raindrops as he held her hand.

But he was relieved, too, because he had a feeling

that with Scarlett Johansson in your arms, you became the enemy of three and a half billion other men. In envying you, they hated you. In hating you, they destroyed you.

He was also relieved because if the New York actress's flamboyant frontage made you want to conjure up grand plans – the texture of her skin, ideas about sex – it was still rather difficult for a young garage mechanic turned Good Samaritan, even if he was like-Ryan-Gosling-only-better-looking, to become Scarlett Johansson's boyfriend (the competition was planetary), while becoming the boyfriend of a girl like Jeanine Foucamprez seemed an ambition considerably more accessible.

And how nice it would be, he thought, if that did happen and as a result you secretly felt you were making love to two women at once, or making love to one of them while thinking of the other, and doing so with total impunity.

But Arthur Dreyfuss knew that he hadn't reached that point yet. Two storeys and a bathroom separated him from Jeanine Foucamprez at night, thirty-nine steps which, he had an idea, it would be difficult for him to climb, because Jeanine Foucamprez was living in a nightmarish fairy tale which made it hard to tell whose body or whose desire was fooling whose, and in cruel fairy tales of that kind, princes don't know how to give the kiss that will bring the princess back to life the next morning, to restore peace, the will to live, and a sense of the sweetness of things. Those are sad and solitary mornings. Mornings of pain. Savage mornings. It takes a wounded princess a long time to heal.

Always the same old story: medicinal drugs. Calculating the dosage. Fingers that tremble.

Of course, he stopped the film they were watching. It hadn't finished yet (for anyone who's interested, here's a quick recap of the ending: Ewan McGregor finally leaves with Scarlett Johansson on a boat bound for . . . an *island* – ah, love), but he stopped the film and Jeanine Foucamprez said: It doesn't matter, I've already seen it. Then there was a moment of silence and slight embarrassment. They looked at each other and you would have thought they were seeing one another for the first time.

All the same; you watch Cameron Diaz in a film, for instance, and it isn't really Cameron Diaz you see. It takes you a while to realise that.

It took Arthur Dreyfuss six minutes.

Why me? he asked. Why my house, why here, why Long?

Jeanine Foucamprez took a deep breath and,

without that wonderful accent this time, she launched into her story.

I work on the Nocesdemiel campaign. I'm one of their top models. I've been doing it for three years. Two towns a day. There are six of us. We act as live models in Nocesdemiel display windows. When there isn't a shop we use a van, glazed all round. In the market place, like fish in an aquarium. Our appearance is announced the day before in the local rag. Sometimes on the France 3 local TV channel. When we arrive there are already people there. It's cheerful. Like a bit of a festival. Carnival time. Plenty of beer, like the selection rounds for Miss France. After the first Nocesdemiel campaign I did, people kept asking for my autograph. I signed Jeanine. They said no, no, sign Scarlett. You're so like her, you're *so*, *so* like her. Please. And I felt beautiful. Important. So I signed myself as Scarlett, with a big S, like Zorro with his big Z. People liked it. They hugged me. The next year they brought me her photo. The cover of a DVD with her on it. A small poster for a film. A page from *Première* magazine. An article from *Elle*. The front cover of a TV magazine. Suddenly, I didn't feel so beautiful. I felt like a liar. A little clown. Six months ago we were leaving Abbeville to go to Amiens, but the driver turned off the motorway because a container truck full of milk had overturned. It looked as if it had been snowing. One of the girls said it was like a wedding dress with bubbles of air forming the pattern of lace. We stopped here, at Long. We had lunch at the brasserie beside the water. I remember every detail. It was Friday, the nineteenth of March. I saw you when we were returning to the minibus. Your hands were all black and your dungarees were dirty. I thought of Marlon Brando in a film about motorbikes. You were repairing a little girl's bike and she was crying. You were handsome. And proud. The light of the little girl's bike came back on and so did her smile. That was what killed me. Her smile.

Arthur Dreyfuss's mouth suddenly went dry. Although he didn't yet know the words of love (even Follain used them sparingly), he felt that here, in this moment, he was hearing words that were meant for him alone, words like kisses coming from those wonderful lips, lips that could easily be those of the troubling Scarlett Johansson, with all that was recognised to be appetising and soft about her, on which it is not necessary to go into further detail.

I ran back to the brasserie and they told me where you lived. The house standing alone on the road from Long to Ailly, just before the motorway.

He drank a mouthful of wine, a second. It was a Ventoux, fruity with an aroma of quince and red fruits,

Tonnelier had said, perfect with charcuterie and pastry rolls filled with cheese.

He felt a little light-headed.

She went on.

If you thought I was her, I knew you'd open the door. I thought I might have a chance. Like the little girl with her bicycle lamp and her killer smile. And . . . oh, shit.

Neither his father, Louis-Ferdinand Dreyfuss, nor his mother, Thérèse Dreyfuss, née Lecardonnel, really had the presence of mind to tell their only son about love.

Mourning for Noiya, his little sister, had taken up most of the time they spent together, until the final 'See you this evening' and the beginning of the vermouth. Thérèse Dreyfuss, née Lecardonnel, cried a lot; every day she seemed to be escaping through her tears. She talked about the things she had lost forever: her little daughter's wet kisses; nursery rhymes; an attack of measles, an attack of chickenpox; having to disentangle Noiya's hair one day when she would have been seven; Mother's Day presents, necklaces made of pasta, appalling poems; dress material to be chosen in the marketplace and dresses to be cut out later, when she was beginning to get breasts; the first drops of perfume dabbed inside her elbows and behind her knees; her first lipstick and her first kiss, her first disappointments – mothers are responsible for those, she said inaudibly, her mouth drowning in liquid grief. Oh, I miss your sister, she told Arthur, I miss her so much. Sometimes I think I can hear her laughing in her room when you and your father have gone out, and then I sit close to her bed, I sing her the songs I never had time to teach her. You're a boy, I didn't sing to you, I didn't read you stories, I wasn't afraid for you, that was your father's role, he was the one who told you about pond-skaters dancing on the dark mirror of the water without ever dipping their long legs in, he was the one who was there to answer your questions, but you never asked any, we thought you weren't interested in anything, we were afraid, oh, Noiya, my baby, my baby, I hate all the dogs in the world, all of them, all of them, even Lassie (*Lassie Come Home*, *Courage of Lassie*, *Challenge to Lassie* – the indefatigable Lassie).

Now and then Louis-Ferdinand Dreyfuss took his son fishing. It would still be dark when they set out. They crossed the marshes, heading towards the pond of Les Croupes or the Planques river and there, near the damp and smelly hut on a little island, the forestry worker, in defiance of municipal rules, fished with a spinner, a lure consisting of a hook and a shiny bit of metal, and he caught several large pike, including one that weighed twenty-one kilos. Was it because his fishing method was illegal, or was it because he didn't want to be seen or heard, that he didn't talk while they were fishing? Arthur Dreyfuss spent hours with his father, in silence, as if he were sitting with a stranger. He used to watch him. He envied him his strong, sure, rugged hands. He watched his clear eyes, in the hope of receiving a smile, a confidence, happiness. He was intoxicated by his father's scent of leather, tobacco and sweat. And sometimes, when the angler ruffled his hair for no particular reason, little Arthur Dreyfuss felt wonderfully happy, and those few seconds of happiness made up for all the silence in the world. All the waiting. All the misery.

One evening in the kitchen, when Arthur Dreyfuss was twelve (Noiya had been eaten six years earlier), he asked his parents how a person fell in love. His father pointed to his mother with his knife, as if to say, she'll tell you. But then a dog began barking in the distance, whereupon his mother burst into tears and took refuge in her bedroom. That evening, for the first time in his life, Arthur Dreyfuss heard his father say sixty-nine words in a row: It's desire, my boy, that's what does it.

Your mother's arse was what attracted me (here the child jumped), her bum if you prefer, the way she had of swaying it as she walked, like the pendulum of a clock, tick, tock, tick, tock. It hypnotised me, I couldn't sleep, so I took her to the little lake of La Bovaque in Abbeville and that's how you came into the world, my boy.

But you did love her, Papa?

Hard to say.

This was the moment when Thérèse Dreyfuss, née Lecardonnel, chose to come out of her room again. Her eyes were dry. They were bloodshot, covered in little red lines, like a cracked vase ready to fall apart. In passing she slapped her husband's face, then took the brown sugar tart out of the oven, and Arthur Dreyfuss had the answer to his question.

My father. He wasn't my real father. Just a pig. A fat pig with a paunch that went *ffft ffft* as he moved. Like wobbling jelly. When he walked it always sounded as if he were wearing wet shoes. Threatening to go into a skid even when it wasn't raining. My real father, on the other hand, was very handsome. I've seen photos. He was fair-haired (the Johansson side of Jeanine Foucamprez, presumably). Muscular. Girls blushed at his smile. Which made my mother jealous. Often. Then she would calm down. Because after all, she was the one who had caught him. She was very beautiful (the Scarlett side of Jeanine Foucamprez, presumably.) But I never knew my real father. He died just after I was born. Burnt to death in a house in Flesselles (12.3 kilometres from Amiens as the crow flies). He was trying to save an old granny's life. It was impossible to prise them apart. You'd have thought they were making love, like in Pompeii. He was a fireman.

My mother met the pig at a dancing class. She dreamed of becoming a dancer, even if she didn't really have the legs for it. Curvy, with high insteps, all of that. But she thought she had what it took. She was working hard on her dancing. She had photos of Pietragalla and Pavlova on the fridge in the kitchen. Nijinsky and Nureyev as well. And a picture of Jorge Donn in Lelouch's *Bolero*. While she was waiting to get the hang of the *contretemps* and the *grand jeté*, she worked as a waitress. She bit her nails to the quick. Dance was just a pretext for Mr Piggy. A way to pick women up. Like Hugh Grant in *About a Boy*. A con artist who pretends he has a kid so he can pick up mothers. As the pig dabbled in photography he took photos: photos of women for their portfolios. In a tutu. Then without a tutu, in transparent tights. Then in close-up. He was such a rotten photographer that he even managed to make my mother look ugly. I was five when he came to live with us. At first he was cool. He helped a bit around the place. He danced with my mother. Tango, cha-cha-cha, mambo. We laughed, my mother and me. He was ridiculous. The only good side was that he could mend things when they went wrong. The toilet flush.

The doorbell. Electric sockets. We were saving money.

He thought I was pretty. He said I had skin like satin that made you want to feel it between your fingers. My eyes were like alexandrites (gemstones that change colour in different lights). He was sad, he said, because there were millions of people who couldn't share his emotion. His joy in looking at me. Beauty is so rare, he said, so lovely. You want to pass it on. That's how it began. A first series of photos, taken in the kitchen. He wanted me to eat vanilla ice cream. He wanted me to have the spoon in my mouth, with the ice cream running down my chin. The look on his face was different from when my mother was around. This is our secret, Jeanine. I felt important. I felt beautiful. It went on. In the garden. He asked me to do a headstand. A cartwheel. Did I know how to do a scissors jump with my legs? One day he came into the bathroom while I was in the tub. He was looking very sad. He told me he'd once had a little girl who had gone to heaven. He said I looked like her, and he hadn't had time to take enough photos of her so that he'd never forget her. And if I'd let him take photographs of me washing myself then he'd never be sad again. My mother came in while I was washing in between my legs the way he'd shown me. I was laughing because it tickled. And he was laughing, too. Yes, yes, like that. She looked at us and then she closed the door. Quietly, without slamming it. And the pig said thank you, thanks to you I'll never forget my little girl. Now I'm going to see your Maman. I didn't hear any shouting in the kitchen. Any broken china. Only silence. She didn't say anything. My mother didn't say anything. She never asked me about it. She didn't want to know, or see. She became blind towards me. She never took me in her arms again.

Arthur Dreyfuss gently took Jeanine Foucamprez in his arms, and this entirely unexpected gesture of affection surprised them both. He felt deeply sad. The anger would come later. He had no words for that grief, that violence; the only thing he could do, the only vocabulary he could draw on, was to hold her close. It was pure and chaste.

It isn't time that civilises us, but the way we live.

It had been dark outside for some time, the moon revealing the shadowy zones of the world, but they did not feel tired. New encounters, or at least those that seem important, always have that effect: you don't feel sleepy, you never want to sleep again, you want to tell the story of your life, all of it, share the songs you love, the books you have read, your lost childhood, your disillusionment, and then that hope – you wish you had always known each other, so that you could embrace and love each other, knowing why, with confidence, waking up in the morning with the impression that you have been together forever and forever, without the bitter pain of dawn.

It was the Ventoux from Tonnelier that got the better of their resistance; Jeanine Foucamprez delicately laid her head against the garage mechanic's shoulder, as you might heave a sigh when you finally arrive somewhere, slightly reassured and slightly warmed; and even if Arthur Dreyfuss's position on the sofa was not as comfortable for him as it might have been, he did not change it, too overwhelmed to find that a girl as beautiful as Scarlett Johansson, suddenly pale and light as a swan's feather, had just put her head on his shoulder.

The daughter of the fair-haired fireman went peacefully to sleep, and the son of the forestry worker who could string sixty-nine words together and whose body had disappeared began to dream.

In the morning, thunderous knocking on the door woke them.

Arthur Dreyfuss had some difficulty extricating himself from the Ektorp sofa because of the terrible cramp paralysing his left shoulder (the one against which the beautiful head of Jeanine Foucamprez had been resting for nearly six hours. She now roused herself, smiling).

It was PP, his face grey, his mouth set in a menacing line.

What the hell do you think you're doing, boy? I've been expecting you for the last hour, the mayor's Mégane is coming in at nine!

Then, spotting Jeanine Foucamprez delicately stretching on the three-seater Ektorp, he looked surprised, then astonished (remember the look on the face of the slavering wolf in Tex Avery's animated cartoon when *Red Hot Riding Hood* passes by?). So all that stuff about the actress wasn't just bullshit? he said, whistling. Wow, who is she, is it really Angelina Jolie? She is completely gorgeous. Oh Jesus. Fucking hell. And for the first time in his life Arthur Dreyfuss felt attractive. Chosen. One of the elect. While for the first time in his life PP, three marriages behind him, two divorces, proprietor of a garage representing several makes of car, let his heart do the talking. Come in a little later, if you like, I understand . . . Marilyn, the raindrops, take it slowly, delicately. I'll look after the Mégane, you look after her.

The moment PP closed the door Jeanine Foucamprez began to smile, then they laughed, laughter that seemed to them synonymous with happiness.

An end to being in limbo. A new beginning. Possibilities. Sincerity.

After a cup of Ricoré instant coffee drunk in haste – leave the washing up, go and help him, I'll clear up, Jeanine Foucamprez said – Arthur hurried to the garage. He'd had an idea. Besides the mayor's Mégane, under which the large body of PP lay stretched, there were three jobs he had to do: the 250,000 km service on a fifth-hand BMW Series 3; fixing the exhaust pipe on a 2005 C1 – a filthy old banger, said PP, designed by one-armed idiots who'd never earned their mechanics' licences; and punctures to be mended on two camper vans. (Whether through ochophobia or kinetophobia – fear of cars or fear of movement to you and me – Jipé, manager of the Grand Pré camping site, one of the two sites at Long, which consisted of small islets separated by streams of water, so that you could fish from your caravan, was in the habit of puncturing a few tyres from time to time, then sending the unfortunate tourists to PP for help in exchange for a 10 euro note).

Each time their eyes met, PP couldn't help winking like an imbecile, like some hammy actor in an old black-and-white film. In their short break at 10 a.m. (usually 9.30) PP literally bombarded Arthur with questions, but received only one answer, always the same: she rang my doorbell, that's all. And PP cursed, saying he was not some mad old hag or a crook, yet things like that, a blonde bombshell knocking on the door, never happened to him, PP, although his look – a bit Gene Hackman, with an attractive face, and a solidly built body like Lino Ventura's – went down pretty well in general, and why couldn't Angelina Jolie have dropped in on him instead, or, let's say, dropped in at the garage, because Julie (his wife) was always in the kitchen, which explained the paunch, or maybe in the shower since I installed a new shower head with five jets; and let me tell you something, Arthur, even if you're not so bad-looking you're only a kid, and to satisfy a woman like that, to give her a really good time, to look after the best interests of a star like that and take her to ecstasy and back, well that takes a real man, someone hefty, because it's the weight, see? It's suffocating and that leads to asphyxia, and asphyxia is erogenous, any lady will tell you that, and you're built like a boy, it's not so much a prick you've got between your legs there as a feather, a little feather, a breath of wind, nothing asphyxiating about that. (A pause here.) Oh shit, shit, bloody shit! He violently stubbed out his cigarette as if it were a large, hairy spider with a white abdomen like a blister full of pus that was about to poison him – Rastapopoulos in *Flight 717 to Sydney*.

Right, get shot of this damn C1, then go home and watch *Tomb Raider*, that's what I'd do if I were you, I wouldn't even have come in to work, you dumb-ass. Go gather your nectar, make her blossom. Spray on some aftershave, think of pretty things to say. Don't miss this chance, you pillock, she's a flower, go pick her. A girl like that, she's a miracle; you'll never be a sad loser again, you'll be envied, desired. Think of Marilyn and me. Marilyn and me . . . I'd die if I were you.

It was now that Arthur Dreyfuss told his boss about

his idea. PP pulled a face. Look, PP, you know, Arthur explained, smiling, my holidays, all the days I haven't taken over these last two years, you said you'd put them aside for when I really needed them. He took a deep breath and then ventured these words: And beauty / Is greater than anything / Greater than a heart. / The dust of immortality / as it fades away.

PP smiled a paternal smile. You're a delicate soul, Arthur, a bit of a poet the way you knit your words together. Go on, then. Take her away, off you go, knock on the doors of heaven. Get your taste of immortality, like you said.

It was 10.30 in the morning of the fourth day. The weather was fine.

Arthur and Jeanine

Jeanine Foucamprez wasn't working at the time.

It was September, and the Nocesdemiel advertising campaigns didn't get going again until January with the new lines of wedding dresses – silky mikado or micro-Ottoman fabric, or pearlised cornelli lace – and everything else that marriage promises: the first sunny days; the desperate sacrifices inflicted on themselves by brides-to-be, the Dukan diet, Nuvoryn pills, gastric bands and other drastic measures to make them beautiful, at least once, in the inevitable photograph.

She had spent two weeks working in the poultry section of a supermarket in Albert (28 kilometres from Amiens, 813 from Perpignan) and although she was sometimes on the receiving end of dubious jokes – *Did you see that pretty little chicken they've put in poultry?* – or just downright vulgar ones – *There's a bird I wouldn't mind stuffing* – in spite of these jokes, Jeanine Foucamprez had liked the work. She wore a costume made of swan's feathers, very soft, with a cordless microphone, and every five minutes she had to recite a little verse: *Here's a chicken, oh, so pretty! Here's a basket, why not fill it with some tasty chicken fillet?* The stock controllers had been very nice to her, a coffee here, a chocolate bar there; so had the manager, buying her dinner at the Royal Picardie, and the accountant, a ride in his new Jaguar XF; of course, there were ulterior motives, dreams, suffering; the usual ugly business she'd known with every man she'd met since she was twelve, with her feminine charms, her mouth like a ripe fruit, that sacred *je ne sais quoi* (although everyone knows what it is) that makes men unhappy, brutal and crazy, and women distrustful, feverish and cruel.

Jeanine Foucamprez never stayed in the same place for long; people accused her, pre-emptively, of pyromania, like that Laurie Bee Cool, the Lauren Bacall lookalike in Bob Clampett's animated cartoon, the girl who leaves fire in her wake and consumes the heart of Bogey Gocart. She was chased as far away as possible because she was a poison, a danger, a siren, daughter of the river god Achelous.

She was a chimera, a dream. There were respectable

clinics where blades cut other faces to make them look like hers. Scalpels carved bodies, refashioning them in her image: big breasts, small waist. Jeanine Foucamprez brought unhappiness to men who couldn't possess her and women who didn't resemble her.

The great waltz of appearances.

If they only knew. The real life of the woman who looked like the character Alex Foreman in the film *In Good Company* was a succession of ugly wounds, small miseries and humiliation.

Her mother's arms had never opened to her again. Her mother's mouth had never uttered loving words. Her hands had never brushed the child's hair again, or touched her or reassured her. And when the first wrinkles appeared at the corners of those blind maternal eyes, and she knew she would never join Pavlova, Nijinsky and Nureyev on the kitchen fridge, would never succeed in performing the *échappé battu* and the *sissonne retirée*, her mother's silence had become even more threatening. Talk to me, Maman, Jeanine had asked, had begged. Say something. Please. I beg you. Open your mouth and let something out. Throw up, if you like, vomit on me, but don't leave me like this. Don't leave me in silence, Maman. People drown in silence, you know they do. Tell me that's not what you want. Tell me I'm still your daughter.

Silence can be as violent as words.

Jeanine Foucamprez was just nine when her mother left her in the care of her aunt, a kind woman married to a postman, living in Saint-Omer. They had no children, which had nothing to do with the fact that he was a postman and she a librarian; they lived in a nice little house with a garden, near the lakes of Malhove and Beauséjour. I grew up with them, Jeanine Foucamprez told the young mechanic. My uncle always left the house early in the morning. He had to, he was a postman. As soon as the postman had gone to deliver his letters, Jeanine and her aunt played Céline Dion's records, with the volume turned right up (*Feliz Navidad! It's All Coming Back to Me Now!*). They danced in the kitchen. In the sitting room. They sang along, descending the stairs like film stars. We laughed, I was happy. Then, at eight o'clock, I went to school and my aunt went to the library. In the evening we read novels, or watched TV, while my uncle, sitting at the kitchen table, tried to write a book about the history of the Saint-Omer canal, beginning with some monks in the tenth century. Boring, but I was happy there. It didn't last.

When she was twelve, the little 'buds, as sweet and pale as Communion wafers', as the photographer had called them, turned into an enormous pair of breasts, tearing her brutally away from the sweetness of childhood and the songs of Céline Dion and delivering her over to the lust of human pigs.

This was how Arthur Dreyfuss's first paid holiday began: with the two of them lying on the floor, since the house had no garden (which explained the reasonable price), on the long-haired rug in the sitting room (from Ikea, 133x195 cm, the size of a small double bed), as happy as if they had been lying on warm grass surrounded by buttercups, as happy as if they had been playing *do you like butter?* with the reflection of the pale petals – a charming game that Arthur Dreyfuss as a child would have liked to play with his little sister, if only the neighbour had had a soft spot for chihuahuas rather than Dobermanns.

Jeanine Foucamprez looked up at the ceiling, smiling as if it were the sky, with its clouds and white birds taking you to the other side of the world, a sky as blue as the blue eyes of lovers from the children's rhyme, and she felt, for a very brief moment, something of the childhood she had never had. The fireman's gentle nature. The dancer's grace. Then, later, adolescence, holding a nice boy's hand – the dream of a simple life, which might perhaps seem naive, but which often contains the key to happiness. She sighed, her chest swelled, but as Jeanine Foucamprez was lying down it did not assume Russ Meyer-like proportions and the garage mechanic did not faint away; her chest heaved once, twice, and then subsided. The nostalgic adolescent in Jeanine confided:

It feels good, being with you.

Then Arthur Dreyfuss's fingers, stiff from remaining still for so long, so close to that extraordinary body, the temple of every sin, came to life like five timid little slow-worms and reached out for the hand whose twin had held the hand of Ewan McGregor; and when they reached their destination, Jeanine Foucamprez's hand opened up, like five soft little petals on a botanical treasure, to receive the fingers of the young man who was like Ryan Gosling, only better-looking.

Ryan-Gosling-only-better-looking then squeezed her hand, brought it towards him, and said, getting to his feet: Come on!

She got to her own feet, indeed jumped to them. Arthur Dreyfuss smiled.

He felt dizzy, as he had on the day when he inhaled trichloroethylene with Alain Roger, who had just lost his virginity, and had sung Vivaldi's *Stabat Mater* although he had never understood a word.

Christiane Planchard owed the fact that she didn't have a heart attack to her good health and the regular practice of yoga.

Christiane Planchard ran the hairdressing salon that bore her name in the Rue Saint-Antoine. The salon also lent out DVDs and received ink and laser cartridges to be refilled. Anyway, but for her regular yoga exercises and the ability to keep her emotions under control, Christiane Planchard would have dropped dead on the spot when she saw Scarlett Johansson (just think, Scarlett Johansson!) coming into her salon alongside the cute young garage mechanic.

That said, just at the moment her mouth opened wide, her scissors also snapped shut, massacring the old-fashioned fringe favoured by Mademoiselle

Thiriard, retired English teacher and confirmed old maid (which perhaps might be explained by the superannuated fringe).

All the gossip, chit-chat and idle talk stopped dead. Time was suspended. You could have heard a pin drop.

What everyone present did hear was the faint click of a smartphone taking a photo, and that tiny sound seemed to be the signal for life to start again. Christiane Planchard hurried forward: Oh, what an honour, Mademoiselle Johansson, you . . . are you making a film in these parts? With Woody Allen? I know he loves France! And he plays the clarinet so well! What beautiful hair you have, so blonde, like a wheat field in spring, like hawkweed in summer, you're . . . you're even more beautiful in real life – but here Arthur Dreyfuss interrupted Christiane. Could you cut her hair short and colour it black, please? At these words Christiane Planchard seemed to sway, but then recovered herself (thanks to the yoga position called the *brujangasana* or *cobra*, which gives you *the self-confidence to overcome all obstacles and the strength you need to face life in general; the idea of it is to visualise blue light level with your throat*). Black, yes, of course, Chantal, could you look after Mademoiselle Johansson? Get the shampoo ready, please, the special shampoo, go on; just a minute, if you please, Mademoiselle Thiriard, I'm sure you can see that I'm . . . yes, yes, your new fringe looks good, very good, it's *destructured*, everyone's asking me for that kind of fringe now. And while everyone busied themselves around the divine actress, Jeanine Foucamprez stood on tiptoe, dropped a kiss on Arthur Dreyfuss's cheek and, with the smile that left three and a half billion men swooning with pleasure, whispered *thank you* in his ear.

Jeanine Foucamprez's heart beat a little faster. She was the one he wanted. Not the other woman.

And while her blonde locks fell casually to the floor, tracing first a golden crown and then a tawny carpet round her, Arthur Dreyfuss spent the time reading dog-eared magazines (with the Sudoku and crossword puzzles filled in, the recipes torn out, and moustaches drawn in ballpoint pen on the face of poor Demi Moore and that guy she was going out with). In an old issue of *Public* he found an article describing the forthcoming release of *Iron Man 2*, starring Robert Downey Jr., Gwyneth Paltrow and . . . Scarlett Johansson in the role of the Black Widow, with long auburn hair, a black dress cinched in at the waist, and as always that amazing figure. He leafed through other popular magazines, read old horoscopes, and found a startling article by a woman who had had a nymphoplasty, also known as a labiaplasty. Until that moment he had always thought that a nymph was a pretty mythological girl, or, as his father had told him, a stage in the metamorphosis of an insect, but now he discovered that some women handed their vaginas over to the scalpels of cosmetic surgeons. *The small labia were hanging down, my vagina looked like an old turkey neck. But since the operation it's been like a girl's, fresh and smooth*. He got gooseflesh.

Lies make their home just about anywhere.

Two hours later – members of staff having gone over to Dédé's chip shop twice to get coffee for Mademoiselle Johansson and her cute friend; theirs was an unpretentious salon, but they knew how to give good service, Christiane Planchard said – two hours later Jeanine Foucamprez emerged as a brunette with tousled hair worn in an urchin cut (for those old enough to remember what that was, rather like Anne Parillaud's style in *Nikita*), and everyone agreed that she was very pretty like that; to be sure, the look was slightly surprising at first, when you were used to seeing her with blonde hair flowing loose or tied up in a chignon, but yes, she was very pretty, even astonishingly pretty with the new hairstyle. Jeanine Foucamprez agreed to pose with Christiane Planchard for a photograph that would be enlarged and framed the next day, to be hung on the wall behind the cash desk.

As they left the salon, she slipped her arm through

Arthur Dreyfuss's and walked out to the sound of applause. To everyone present that day, the image of that improbable, beautiful couple seemed radiant, almost like an apparition, and no one could have suspected the violent darkness that would sweep it all away – in what was now less than forty-eight hours' time.

That seventh day was an ill-omened day, black and purple.

They walked to the garage, where they borrowed the 'courtesy car' (an old Honda Civic) from PP, and PP in his turn could not help paying a compliment: You're even more beautiful than you were yesterday, Mademoiselle Angelina. Jeanine Foucamprez gave him an exquisite smile.

Arthur Dreyfuss drove cautiously as they went the thirty-two miles from Long to Amiens, where he had booked a table at the Relais des Orfèvres, because he and Jeanine talked a lot and conversation is always something of a distraction when you're behind the wheel.

It was kind of you to think of going to the hairdresser's, she said.

It really suits you, he said.

Do you think so?

Yes.

She blushed. So did he.

Where are you taking me?

It's a surprise.

I love surprises.

I hope you'll like this one.

I'm sure I will. I'm so glad I spotted you last March. You were so good-looking.

Oh, stop!

So touching, with that little girl. And her laugh. Her laugh was really great. It made me think of you almost every day. You must think I'm an idiot.

No, I don't.

I dreamed of meeting you. And of you making me laugh like that little girl.

Okay then, maybe you are an idiot.

Let's be friends.

Let's . . .

And so on, for thirty-two kilometres.

It was adolescent banter, charming, patient: the moment *before*, when everything is possible; words simply placed there, in no particular order, words that precede the writing.

There was no haste in Arthur Dreyfuss's demeanour, no provocation in Jeanine's, and when she put her hand to her short hair, when she became acquainted with her new look, there was something discreet in her gestures, something touching that filled the driver with happiness. When they arrived at the famous restaurant, she put her hand on his forearm.

Thank you for trying to get rid of Scarlett for me, Arthur. For coming to meet me, trying to see me . . . and I mean *me*.

Arthur Dreyfuss smiled, and didn't say anything, because there was nothing more to be said.

At the Relais des Orfèvres, the restaurant run by the chef Jean-Michel Descloux, they ordered the traditional menu. It cost 30 euros, but still, thought the modest mechanic, when you're taking out a girl like this – a Marilyn Monroe, PP had said, mixing her up with Angelina Jolie – you say yes, thank you, we'll have the traditional menu. You tell yourself: I might die tomorrow. In fact, I might die this very minute. You tell yourself that money doesn't matter. *Carpe diem*, you think.

(The traditional menu, for real gourmets, was as follows. First course: a crusty timbale of fillet of smoked black pollock with creamed cauliflower; main course, roast hake with seaweed butter, crisp ham tuiles with *piquillo* sauce – made with a kind of sweet pepper grown in Lodosa in the Spanish Basque region – and finally, Julien Planchon's cheese trolley *or* the dessert menu. The economic miracle of those 30 euros was contained in that 'or'.)

Of course, the other guests glanced over at them. Glanced over, in particular, at her. Pointed at them, more or less discreetly. The other guests whispered, excited, but Arthur Dreyfuss put their reaction down to boredom. They were just an ordinary, if good-looking, young man accompanied by a very pretty woman, looking at the other women. Other men's wives and girlfriends. Trophies.

Always this great waltz.

Jeanine Foucamprez had pink, pearly cheekbones like Scarlett Johansson's, and although her hairstyle made her look radically different, it had to be admitted that the resemblance to the actress was still there. Heaven knows Arthur Dreyfuss thought she was beautiful. She was finally unique: no one had ever seen her like this before, not with that expression of almost childish delight on her face. Like many other men at that moment, he would happily have died to take the place of that little spoon of creamed cauliflower that she was raising to her luscious lips, putting into her mouth, and withdrawing as shiny as a film star's tears; after all, hadn't Woody Allen dreamed of being Ursula

Andress's tights? I've never eaten anything as good as this, cried Jeanine Foucamprez, moved, her eyes moist. Except once, perhaps, when I was having a *ficelle picarde* at the Royal Picardie hotel with the manager of the supermarket when I was working there. (Again, for the gourmets mentioned above, the *ficelle picarde* is an oven-cooked pancake filled with ham and mushrooms, 420 calories per 100 grams.) But it was so embarrassing, she went on. He ate so fast and kept giving me funny looks. He was sweating. He wanted to know if I'd ever seen the bedrooms in thc Royal. Hc said that it would do me good to have a little rest after dinner, to help my digestion. After all, a *ficelle picarde* is rather a heavy dish, like a cheese gratin. And so on and so forth. The manager weighed about ten tons. Married. With two grown-up daughters. And a man like that goes running after girls the same age as his daughters. Arthur Dreyfuss was about to ask a question, but she silenced him with a shrug of her shoulders and added with a smile, the little spoon brushing those magical lips: Come on, Arthur, what do you think? I don't go to bed with someone just for a *ficelle picarde*. The guy smiled, he was a smooth talker. You have such a nice mouth, two beautiful . . . and that's it, off they go, they think they can take all kinds of liberties. I get to see the worst sort, Arthur. Men in a hurry, clumsy men, handsome men, even very handsome men. Old men, mean men, bastards and creeps. They've all tried it on with me. Flowers, chocolate, *ficelles picardes*, money. A lot of money. Insults, too. Oh, but I couldn't imagine their suffering! A diamond ring once, but not the proposal of marriage to go with it. Just an apartment later on. Like a tart. Oh, and a Fiat 500 with a leather interior. Men! I could even choose the colour. But I've never met anyone who was kind. Really kind. You're the first, Arthur. And kindness overwhelms a girl, because it doesn't ask for anything in return.

The heart of Arthur Dreyfuss almost skipped a beat. He was about to place his rough hand, capable of dismantling any engine in the world (and perhaps someday the hearts of mankind) and putting it back together again, on the lightly dimpled hand of Jeanine Foucamprez, when a small voice, very close to them, spoke up.

Could I have your autograph, please, Scarlett?

A plump little girl was standing beside their table. She was holding out the menu to Jeanine Foucamprez for her to sign and looking at the New York actress with eyes full of love and devotion, like the eyes of a wet dog, a basset hound, full of submission and veneration.

The child was going on:

I've already got the autographs of Jean-Pierre

Peraud and the Fatals Picards [who represented France, unsuccessfully, in the 2007 Eurovision Song Contest]. But I haven't got the autograph of a great actress like you.

Tears welled up in the lovely eyes of Jeanine Foucamprez; she put her hands to the short, dark hair that did not hide the amazing actress's identity; the frightened little fan suddenly flinched and backed away as the actress rose abruptly, her chair fell over, and she fled in tears. The child's lips were trembling as she asked: What did I do wrong? But Arthur Dreyfuss also rose to his feet, threw some money on the table – he had seen someone do that in *The Sopranos* – and ran after Jeanine Foucamprez as if in pursuit of happiness itself.

She was sitting outside, on the bonnet of the courtesy car.

Arthur Dreyfuss really had no words for a situation such as this. Capable as he was of reassuring a woman in tears because her car wouldn't start, or soothing her when a distributor cap had come off, he was unable to repair the grief of a girl who was crying because another woman, in America, was inundating her, stealing away her life. He ventured to put out his hand. Dared to caress her short, urchin-cut hair, to wipe away, as if they were watercolour, the drops of mercury falling from her eyes. He tried to breathe calmly, warmly, like a real man, like PP – a steady breathing in which she might abandon herself, feel at peace, far, far away from the *other* woman.

It took Jeanine Foucamprez several minutes to calm down. Then she locked her eyes on Arthur's and unspoken words were exchanged. She gently slid off the bonnet of the car, stood on tiptoe and grew taller, grew until her velvety lips met the lips of Ryan Gosling, only better-looking.

That was their first real, loving kiss.

That wonderful kiss soon took Arthur Dreyfuss's mind off the disappointing scene in the restaurant. His heart took wing, his soul was gambolling. He was Bambi.

As he drove, with the wonderful Jeanine Foucamprez beside him, he sang along at the top of his voice with the song that was coming over the car radio: *With love you must not play, / Not even for a day. / I never can forget / the tears you shed, and yet / a thoughtless word, a single glance / can spell the end to our romance*. It was an old song by Valdo Cilli (born in 1950, in Italy, came to Roubaix in 1958, became a singer in a dance hall and at other evening events, had his moment of glory in the first part of the show put on by Gérard Lenorman, was struck down by a heart attack in Roubaix in 2008 – the cruelty of the northern climate); the girl who had worked in the poultry section laughed and laughed, and both of them, tiptoeing carefully into the cotton-wool fields of attraction and desire, looked very beautiful in that moment.

After the slushy Valdo Cilli song, Jeanine Foucamprez said she wanted to stop off at Saint-Omer to introduce the garage mechanic to her aunt – the childless librarian, wife of a postman bent on writing a book about the Saint-Omer canal. And since the hospital where Arthur Dreyfuss's mother now lived was on the way, they agreed to call in and see her, too. Make introductions, like promises.

A few years earlier Thérèse Dreyfuss, née Lecardonnel, had been admitted to Abbeville hospital, which specialised in treating all kinds of psychiatric problems: alogia, alienation, hallucinations, psychoses and other disorders, phantoms and cannibalistic anxieties.

It is true that the regular and heavy consumption of alcohol (vermouth in this case) can cause Wernicke's encephalopathy, a form of alcoholic dementia, or Korsakoff syndrome. The latter had been diagnosed in Noiya's inconsolable mother.

Thérèse Dreyfuss, née Lecardonnel, was suffering, it was decided, from anterograde amnesia, disorientation, mythomania (an inclination to fantasise) and anosognosia (lack of awareness of her own illness). She would also be diagnosed as having a tendency to euphoria, but with absent reflexes and sometimes a breakdown in language.

They arrived about three in the afternoon.

She was sitting on a bench in the garden and her head was nodding like the heads of those plastic dogs you see on the rear shelf of certain cars. There was a rug over her knees, although the weather was still mild. Arthur Dreyfuss went and sat down beside her. Jeanine Foucamprez stayed in the background; she knew about the oceans that can lie between a mother and her child. Arthur's mother said, without even turning her head to her son: I've already had my biscuit and my apple, I'm not hungry now, I'm full.

It's me, Maman.

The dogs aren't hungry either. Not any more. They're all full. Obese. They've eaten my children.

It's me, Arthur, whispered Arthur Dreyfuss. I'm your son.

Oh, stop that, Georges. You can't seduce me. I'm empty. No heart left. Heart swallowed, she said, giving a sharp shudder and still not looking at her son. Stop, my husband will be here soon. He'll be angry. My husband. Gone. Where's his body? The dog is eating. (Who is Georges?)

Jeanine Foucamprez met Arthur's eyes. There was a sad smile on her face, a smile on the verge of tears. She's talking, she said. At least she's talking to you.

Arthur Dreyfuss gently perched his hand on his mother's shoulder like a little bird. Still she did not move. He felt very emotional and was angry with himself for not having come to see her sooner, for continually putting off this visit because of an oil change, a service, a dirty spark plug on a moped – because you always leave those you love until last. He suddenly understood the vanity of things, and faced with his mother, whose mind was wandering in ethereal and dangerous places, he knew he was a bad son and shame pierced his heart like a dagger.

I came to say hello, Maman. To find out how you're doing. I can tell you some tales if you want. Tell you what I'm up to now, if you're interested. And there's someone I'd like you to meet. I'll wait a little while with you for Papa –

At these words Thérèse Dreyfuss, née Lecardonnel, turned her head slowly to look at her son. Then she smiled. It was not a pleasant smile. Every other tooth in her mouth was missing and the sturdy survivors were a waxy colour. It was a shock. At the age of forty-six, Thérèse Dreyfuss, née Lecardonnel, was a worn-out old woman. Even after fifteen years, Inke, the murderous Dobermann, was still shredding her heart, her guts and her soul to pieces.

But suddenly her grimace gave way to a wonderful smile, like that of a simple-minded child, a village idiot witnessing marvels; her finger shook as it pointed at Jeanine Foucamprez, who stood two steps away from her, and in a stumbling voice she exclaimed:

Oh, Louis-Ferdinand, look beside you, it's Elizabeth Taylor! She's so beautiful. Oh, so beautiful!

Elizabeth Taylor gently went over to the old lady of forty-six, knelt down in front of her, took her hands in her own and hugged her.

They reached Saint-Omer just as the municipal library was about to close. Jeanine Foucamprez skipped about like a little lamb when she spotted her aunt arranging books on the Children and Young Adults shelves: Roald Dahl, Grégoire Solotareff, Jerome K. Jerome. Then she ran towards her and the childless librarian flung her arms open wide, giving vent to a tremendous, joyful, booming *Jeanine!*

Arthur Dreyfuss smiled sadly as he thought of his own mother, locked inside her embattled body, sitting on her wretched bench – his own mother, who didn't recognise him any more, and would never utter a tremendous, joyful, booming cry of *Arthur!*

After hugging and kissing like the characters in Claude Lelouch's film *A Man and Woman* (*My little*

Jeanine! Auntie! Jeanine darling! Auntie dear!), Jeanine Foucamprez put out her hand to Arthur Dreyfuss. I'd like you to meet Arthur, Auntie.

Her auntie gave her a mischievous smile and Jeanine Foucamprez blushed slightly. My boyfriend, Auntie, Arthur Dreyfuss.

The moment she said this, the librarian's mischievous expression vanished, her mouth formed a circle, a kind of capital *O*, and she started muttering the boyfriend's name almost inaudibly. Arthur Dreyfus. You're Arthur Dreyfus? The librarian looked as if she were about to faint. Arthur Dreyfus? Then she disappeared, taking small, delicate steps.

Arthur Dreyfuss's heart was racing. What had he said? Did she think he was someone else? Had he reminded her of an unpleasant memory? A buried sorrow, some shadow from the past? A lie she had told herself? He remembered the guy from Paris he had met on the Grand Pré campsite (one tyre of the 1986 white Saab 900 and another tyre on his Caravelair Venicia 470 had unfortunately, and simultaneously, had punctures), who kept telling anyone who would listen that his wife looked like Romy Schneider. People were always stopping him in the street to marvel at the resemblance – indeed, that very morning the village hairdresser had done so, a lady called Plumard or Placard, and that was good to hear, because he thought the German actress was the most gifted, brilliant and beautiful woman of all time, and PP had then asked the guy what the hell he thought he was doing, holidaying in a dingy caravan on a rotten camping site, damp and plagued by mosquitoes, where tyres mysteriously got punctured, because if she really was as beautiful as all that then he, PP, would have taken the Romy Schneider lookalike to sit beneath a mangrove or a flame tree, to a blue lagoon where she could bathe naked, yes sir, to a green island with cool waterfalls. (*In the water / there's the radiance of love*, whispered Arthur.) Because if appearances mean so much to you, PP went on, you must respect her, flatter her, make everything around her nice, Mister Parisian, like a frame or a backdrop, yes, that's what I think. If not, you have to see people as they really are, not as you dream them to be. Here the Parisian, his feelings injured, had showed them a photo of his wife on his mobile phone, and neither PP nor Arthur Dreyfuss nor even the notary's wife (who came along to see if by any chance PP was there or more exactly *if he wasn't there*) recognised a Romy Schneider on the little screen. More like a younger Denise Fabre, exclaimed the notary's wife, or Chantal Goya without her hair, added PP; look, she's a bit like Marie Myriam if you take a quick glance, and the Parisian had quickly pocketed his phone. You're going too far, he said, she *does* look like her, even Monsieur Jipé on the campsite said so.

The librarian was back again, holding out a book, her eyes suddenly shining. Her hands were shaking a little. Are you *this* Arthur Dreyfus?* she asked.

No.

Even if he had been tempted for a fleeting moment by the headiness of the dream: No, he said, I'm not that Arthur Dreyfus. My name is spelt with a double *s* and I'm a mechanic. *My hands / don't write the words*. Jeanine Foucamprez came over and took the book. What's this? Her aunt smiled and apologised for her homophonic mistake. Oh, how stupid of me, for a moment I thought you were him, I thought you *could* be him, doing research on a character for your next novel, playing the role of a mechanic. I'm so sorry.

What are you talking about? asked Jeanine Foucamprez, her voice louder this time.

I've dreamed of meeting an author for so long, her aunt went on, a *real* author, not necessarily a very famous one, but authors never come here, this town is too small, too damp, too far from anywhere, and I have

* On 18 February 2010, seven months before these incidents, *La Synthèse du camphre*, the first novel of one Arthur Dreyfus (with one *s*), was published by Gallimard.

no budget to pay the expenses for an author to visit, only a meal at less than 5 euros, you can't even get the dish of the day for that, a sandwich costs more than a paperback, I know everyone has to eat, but we need to dream as well, sixty centimetres of rain fall here each year, the average temperature is barely ten degrees, people are sick of the sight of the Sandelin Museum's pottery, but an author, that makes you dream, words seem gracious again, and suddenly the daily grind, the rain and those ten degrees become poetry.

After a brief handshake / he left on his travels / leaving only things behind.[*]

* Jean Follain, 'Friendship', *Exister* (Gallimard, 1947).

You were within one letter of being a writer, murmured Jeanine, with a bleak smile. You were someone else. Just like me.

Night was falling. They had gone back on the road after saying goodbye to Jeanine's aunt outside the Audomarois municipal library. Jeanine's aunt had set off on her bike, which she used every day whatever the weather forecast (out of solidarity with her husband, the postman and scribbler engaged on the history of the Upper and Lower Meldyck canals, now the Saint-Omer canal).

Jeanine Foucamprez was sitting huddled up in the courtesy car, both feet on the seat, as you sometimes sit when you need to recover your composure. Or simply when you're feeling cold inside.

I wanted to go to the United States and meet her. I'd have liked her to see herself. To imagine what my life might be like with her face. Her mouth, her cheekbones, her breasts. I thought it might be scary for her, too; I mean, having a double. Finding out that she's not unique. It's not all that unusual. *Esquire* magazine named her '*the sexiest woman alive*'. (She gave him a bitter smile.) I'm the sexiest woman alive, Arthur. The sexiest woman and I have the shittiest life. What makes her any different from me? The fact that I was born two years after her? Two years too late? That she's the light and I'm the shade? Why don't we swap lives?

Outside, the bare fields where they'd be sowing wheat in a month's time stretched on, interminable. A few heavy drops of rain on the windscreen, but the thunderstorm didn't break.

In the end I didn't go. What would I have done over there? Listened to people telling me to stop looking like her? To get a nose job. Remodel my mouth. Wear coloured contact lenses, Miss Country Bumpkin. Change my skin colour. Have breast reduction surgery. Off you go. Stop looking like her. Find your true self. Your own little soul. Don't hang around here, clear off. Just stop looking like her, you're doing her harm. Look like someone else if you want to. Look like . . .

Arthur Dreyfuss thought of the faces he'd sometimes seen in magazines, or in Galeries Lafayette in Amiens, women who, in their attempts to look like other people, had had their cheekbones whittled away, or had molars taken out to get a hollow-cheeked look, who'd had their lips filled with Botox to make them seem voluptuous, or had their eyelids tugged about like a blind drawn over their lost youth and vanished illusions. And then it suddenly occurred to him that the pink-cheeked freshness of Jeanine Foucamprez was where real beauty lay: her self-esteem.

As I said, in the end I didn't go. Suppose they'd felt sorry for me? Because maybe I'm some kind of monster. Suppose they'd offered me work as her double. Her shadow. The shadow of her shadow, like in the Jacques Brel song. I'd have been sent off to dine at Balthazar's or the Mercer hotel and be pursued by the paparazzi while she went to visit a new boyfriend in secret. I'd have been standing in for her in sex scenes. She's not too keen on that in her films. She has a no-nudity clause. We have almost the same measurements, you know. Hers are 36-23-34, mine are 35-24-36. I can't even find a decent job looking the way I do, Arthur. I'm good enough to appear in ads in minimarkets or to model wedding dresses, and there's no man who doesn't try to pinch my bum or get me into bed to see what it feels like to screw Scarlett Johansson. Sorry, I'm being vulgar. Because I'm sad.

Arthur Dreyfuss was sad, too.

What would you do if you were her?

Jeanine unfolded the body that felt like her own again and smiled at last.

Well, that's a stupid question. But it's funny. Right then. One, I'd kill myself to give Jeanine Isabelle Marie Foucamprez, that is to say me, a peaceful life, once and for all. Two, I'd burn all the copies of *A Love Song for Bobby Long*, because I think her performance sucks. Three, I'd try to make a record with Leonard Cohen. Four, and a film with Jacques Audiard. Five, I'd stop putting my name to ads that make people think you look more beautiful with, for instance, a Louis Vuitton bag or a L'Oréal face cream. Six, I'd tell little girls that it's not beauty that's good, but desire, and if they're scared there's always a song that can save their lives. Seven, I'd make a record of all those songs. Eight, I'd produce a film for my big sister Vanessa and I'd spoil my mother all the way to infinity! Nine, I'd tell people to re-elect Barack Obama in two years' time. And ten, as I'd be very, very rich with all my starring roles, I'd book a ticket on a flight – a first-class ticket, my dear. I'd drink Taittinger Comtes de Champagne all the way through the flight. I'd nibble on caviar. And I'd come here. I'd cut my career short like Grace Kelly did, and I'd stay with you. If that's what you wanted.

Arthur Dreyfuss was deeply moved.

He stopped the car by the side of the road, left the engine running and looked at her. She was beautiful and her eyes were shining; tears were rising to the mechanic's eyes, too, and he said thank you. *Thank you*. Because if even Follain himself did not use the term in his wonderful assemblages, then it must be a precious one, rare, a term of great beauty that had no need of anything but itself. And at that precise moment, Arthur Dreyfuss wanted something rare.

Later, when they were back on the road, he felt as if he had aged.

They arrived in the middle of the night. Jeanine Foucamprez was dozing on the passenger seat. They crossed Long to reach Arthur Dreyfuss's little house on the D32, on the outskirts of the village.

They had stopped on the way to fill up with petrol and took advantage of the stop to drink a proper coffee and eat a cellophane-wrapped sandwich, soft and unhealthy, with crumbs that stuck to the roof of their mouths. A sandwich for the toothless, he had said, and she had smiled, and then they had thought of his mother and suddenly felt they were being cruel.

Once in the house, Jeanine Foucamprez had dropped a light kiss on his cheek: Thank you, Arthur, for a lovely day. I haven't felt so good since the days when I used to sing *My Heart Will Go On* (the theme tune of *Titanic*) on the stairs with my aunt – and then she went upstairs to her room where she collapsed on the bed, worn out by fatigue and emotion.

Arthur Dreyfuss sat down on the sofa where he had been sleeping for the last four nights, but he didn't go to sleep.

Why had Jeanine Foucamprez, under the magnificent features of Scarlett Johansson, come into his life? She had thought him attractive, cute, she'd said so that first evening, *You're so cute, so cute*; she had wanted to see him again after he had mended a child's bike, and she had arrived just like that, as night was falling four days ago, with her fake Vuitton Murakami bag and a few other things, not enough to last her a week; they had kissed once, a kiss to stop her trembling or shedding tears after Scarlett Johansson had come back to haunt her in the restaurant – but there was no engagement yet. He had thought her attractive (Scarlett Johansson, all the same!), but Jeanine Foucamprez also attracted him. He liked the flaws in her porcelain facade. Her lapses. All those broken things inside her, like there were broken things inside him. Perhaps those things, as Follain wrote, *waiting for writing to deliver them*.* But afterwards. After.

* Jean Follain, 'Appearances', *Des heures* (Gallimard, 1960).

What would life be like afterwards, with a Scarlett Johansson on your arm who isn't Scarlett Johansson but people think is Scarlett Johansson until common sense dictates otherwise, because Scarlett Johansson can't be simultaneously at the presentation of the Nobel Peace Prize in Oslo, Norway, with Michael Caine *and* in the village of Long, France; common sense tells you she can't be saying her lines for three months in Arthur Miller's *A View from the Bridge* at the Cort Theater in New York (138 West 48th Street) and be discussing the freshness or otherwise of a gilt-head bream in the Écomarché in Longpré-les-Corps-Saint. What would that be like?

What would life be like afterwards with Scarlett Johansson? At first you're just her new boyfriend and, furthermore, entirely unknown; then one of the paparazzi tracks you down to the beach at Étretat or Le Touquet, his telephoto lens discovers a birthmark on your left leg, level with the psoas major, ten centimetres under your behind, and once the picture is published *Pointe de Vue* will marvel at this sign of nobility, *Voici* will voice suspicions about a love bite and *Oops* about the possibility of skin cancer. And so the lies begin.

Is reality the essence of a woman or her flesh? Images were jostling one another in his head. He imagined a body as if it were something like a coat. You could take it off, hang it up, leave it on a hook when it doesn't suit you any more. Choose another, one that fits you better, revealing the silhouette of your soul with more precision and elegance. The size of your heart. But there's no such thing; instead of taming it, teaching it a new vocabulary, new gestures, it is cut up, using large-bladed scissors, pinned, and sewn back together again. Its nature is distorted. The coat doesn't look like anything any more, it's just a rag, a pathetic piece of chamois leather. So many frantic women dream of looking different. Looking like themselves but better, maybe. However, all the unhappiness and lies are still there. They never leave you. Like an artificial nose in the middle of your face. When you abandon yourself, you always lose yourself, too. He guesses the weight of women's bodies, the weight of their grief, because Jeanine has talked to him about hers. But you are beautiful in your sorrow, Jeanine. You don't understand the misfortune of ugly women who know themselves to be beautiful, but who are killed slowly, by every scornful look, bit by bit. You don't understand the weight of thick bodies that feel themselves to be bird-like. With plumage. Perfumed. We ought to be seen as we see ourselves: in the kindly light of our self-esteem. He smiles. He feels words growing, arranging themselves in order to trace the way the world is changing. He feels joyful. He wonders whether it isn't Jeanine's fragility that moves him most, even more than her miraculous body.

The softness of a trembling leaf,* Follain wrote. The softness of a trembling leaf. Your incredible softness, Jeanine; the fragility that has the gift of making PP pleasant, elegant even, in the images conjured up by his words; the gift of making Christiane Planchard and all the girls in her salon graceful and light as fairies around you. Your softness that appeases: an encounter with you makes a person feel moved, overwhelmed – 'Beauty is troubling,' Chantal the shampoo girl whispered to me when you saw your short hair and you felt like crying – an encounter with you makes people more tolerant. Chantal added, 'But beauty is dangerous, too, it attracts those things that can destroy it,' and I understood that your softness can both do good and cause harm, like a weapon, words badly put together: for instance, on that night at the petrol station when that stupid arsehole, vulgar and foul-smelling, talked to you as if you were a tart because a lot of guys think a woman with large breasts is bound to be a tart.

Arthur Dreyfuss had almost punched that fetid

* Jean Follain, 'To Slow Things', *Exister* (Gallimard, 1947).

arsehole, but Jeanine Foucamprez had stopped him, saying, 'Leave him alone, you'll only get your hands dirty,' and Arthur Dreyfuss had liked that reply. He had felt that he mattered to her. And that was the most disconcerting thing of all.

With Scarlett Johansson in your arms – well, Jeanine Foucamprez – you wouldn't be the same man. You'd be hers. You'd be *her* man. And women and men would stare at you, sometimes in a friendly way, often sternly, wondering why *you*, what it was about you that was so different, what did you have that they didn't have?

And when they finally found the answer, it would sometimes make them feel unhappy, and sometimes make them cruel.

You were depriving them of her.

Arthur Dreyfuss finally fell asleep on the sofa just as Jeanine Foucamprez was coming down from her room. Outside, the fifth day of their life was breaking.

Jeanine Foucamprez picked up the blanket – it had slipped to the floor – and gently covered the mechanic's body as a mother would, and she shivered to think that ever since she was nine – she remembered the bathtub and the piggish photographer – her mother had never hugged her or tried to warm her up. That she had never cried in her arms again, had never been a little girl again.

She heated water and made a Ricoré instant coffee (they hadn't bought any real coffee yet; they hadn't been shopping together the way two people do when they are living together in the same house); she dipped two pieces of crispbread in it (without butter or jam, for the same reason as above, and because a young man of twenty who lives alone isn't necessarily his own best friend in culinary matters).

Then she looked at him.

Ever since the day when the milk tanker had overturned on the A16 motorway, covering it in white and forcing the driver of the Nocesdemiel campaign bus to go a different way, a route that took them to the village of Long and her destiny, Jeanine Foucamprez had been in love with him, filled with nostalgia for the little girl's laughter.

The moment she saw him she liked everything about him. The way he walked, his clumsy body in dungarees too large for him, his hands black with oil, like shiny leather gloves, so strong, they seemed to her (not for nothing was he the son of the forestry-worker-cum-poacher, the free-loading angler), his handsome face, almost feminine at times, without a trace of arrogance in it (he didn't even seem to know that he was handsome), his candour. Yes, she had felt a little silly that day, a young girl landing at the end of the end of the world (Long, pop. 687, village in Picardy, 9.19 sq. km., part of the canton of Crécy-en-Ponthieu where the famous Battle of Crécy was fought on 26 August 1346, a massacre in which thousands of French died, killed by the archers of King Edward III), arriving at the end of the journey at a place where, with a little luck, she could finally disappear with a nice man (a really nice man, and the child gave him a blessing with her laughter), forget

Scarlett Johansson, forget the cruelty of men, the cowardice of men, their sordid propositions.

Forget the body of the child carved up by the camera lens. The indecency of it. The close-ups. The genitalia, the ultra-fine incision, like a hair. Betrayal by those who were supposed to love you. Abandonment, fear. I hated you all those years, Maman. I hated your silence. He made me feel sick. Made me cut my own skin. Harm myself. I drove needles into my lips. I wanted to silence myself. Like you did. I prayed he would leave you for a thousand sluts of my age. I wanted you to be dead. Alone. For you to be ugly and smell of lard. Tell me that you love me, Maman, if only a little. Tell me I'm clean. Tell me I'll have a nice life. Here, take my hands. I've learnt the waltz, the polka, the carmagnole, I can teach you those dances, Maman. Let's both dance. I miss your kisses. The sound of your voice.

Forget the medicines that dull the mind, liquefy it. Get rid of the desire to swallow a whole box of them and then go to sleep, like beautiful Marilyn Monroe, disturbing Dorothy Dandridge. To sleep and cease there, at the dawn of grace. To dilute yourself like a watercolour. To fade away, fly away, fly back to the warm arms of the fair-haired fireman, somewhere in the sky, and let all your tears flow at last. I have enough tears to fill a river. So much water, enough to put out all the fires in the world, to keep you from burning, dear Papa. To keep you from dying. Don't you leave me as well. Men are bad, bad, and to make them disappear, I must disappear. I must hurt myself, Papa. I hurt.

One night there was going to be an end, without the chance of any dawn, as Céline Dion sang her moving song, 'Fly Little Wing', on the radio: *Fly, fly little wing / Fly beyond imagining / The softest cloud, the whitest dove / Upon the wind of heaven's love / Past the planets and the stars /Leave this lonely world of ours/ Escape the sorrow and the pain / And fly again*. Jeanine Foucamprez had spat out the tablets that were already beginning to choke her, the poison that was carrying her away, sleepy and indolent – the eight grams of Immenoctal, the fifty tablets of Dramamine, according to the recipe in the forbidden book.*

She vomited up her disgust with everything: the horror, the darkness.

A song had caught her. A song had broken her fall and that night Jeanine Foucamprez had seen where safety lay: she must go back there, back to the place where she had seen him.

* Guillon and le Bonniec, *Suicide: A User's Manual* (Éditions Alain Moreau, 1982).

Her angel.

She arrived in Long the next evening. At 19.47 precisely she knocked on Arthur Dreyfuss's door, exhausted, her hair dirty and with dark rings round her eyes. But alive.

Jeanine, Scarlett and Arthur

PP telephoned them to give them a few minutes' warning.

It's the mayor! He's arrived at the garage with a journalist and an old bat with a haircut like Björk's!

(Probably Mademoiselle Thiriard, whose sexagenarian fringe had been massacred when Christiane, startled by the sudden arrival of the world-famous actress in her little hairdressing salon, had let her scissors slip.)

I told them that you would probably be at home and they set off running, even the old lady. They're on their way. Right, I'll leave you to it!

He hung up. Arthur Dreyfuss made a face, Jeanine Foucamprez shrugged her shoulders and said, with a pretty smile: This sort of thing happens all the time. I drive people nuts.

There was a knock on the door.

Leave it to me, Arthur. And she went to let the visitors in.

On the doorstep stood Gabriel Népile, mayor of Long (2008–2014), a journalist from the *Courrier Picard* (local news, Amiens and district), and Mademoiselle Thiriard, retired teacher of English. All three opened their mouths at the mind-boggling sight – for their minds were well and truly boggled – of Scarlett Johansson, looking divine in a man's shirt (property of Arthur Dreyfuss), with her bare legs smooth and graceful, her high cheekbones shining, a cup of Ricoré instant coffee in her hand.

Hello, she said in perfect English.

Mademoiselle Thiriard spoke up in her sexagenarian voice to inform her companions that the actress had just wished them a good day.

So we guessed, murmured the mayor.

What can I do for you? asked the brunette star, better known in her blonde incarnation, in English.

Mademoiselle Thiriard translated again: She wants to know what she can do for us.

Let me introduce myself: I am Gabriel Népile, mayor of this village, and it's an honour to have you staying here with us.

Oh, I you thank, said the actress, switching to clumsy French.

This is Madame Rigodin, a local journalist, and Mademoiselle Thiriard here is acting as our interpreter.

Nice you to see.

Would you be willing to answer a few of Madame Rigodin's questions?

With of pleasure.

Madame Scarlett Johansson, are you in Long for a private visit or in preparation for a film?

I visit Arthur my friend.

I see. So you mean that Monsieur Dreyfuss, our apprentice garage mechanic, is a friend of yours?

Your interpreter do she translate what I say?

Do you mean he is your boyfriend?

I am in marriage.

To Monsieur Reynolds, yes, we know. Well, so, Monsieur Dreyfuss is not your boyfriend. What films are you working on?

We Bought a Zoo, director is Cameron Crowe, and *The Avengers*, director is Joss Whedon. Also I will sing in the Cameron film.

How interesting.

And I prepare my third disc maybe with Peter Yorn this time. And if you want to know all, I sort my rubbish. I try to eat organic but I am not convulsive with the organic (here the interpreter was at a loss). I am not pregnant. In my opinion I have two kilos to lose.

I do not have my sex entirely bare because I think that is like porn star, without the hair is like a piece of beef, yuk, and I like very much the hair or the fleece (here the interpreter hesitated) of Maria Schneider in *Last Tango in Paris* and . . . Oh, your face, it is all red.

Ah? Er . . . I . . . I . . . What do you like about our village in particular?

The garage of the cars. And Arthur.

Will you be staying here long?

I must be in Los Angeles the September twenty-two.

Thank you. I think that's all I wanted to ask, Mayor, said Madame Rigodin.

Mademoiselle Johansson, would you be kind enough to take part in a little film about our lovely village, showing you walking around it with us? It's for the village hall internet site. We could show you our lovely Louis XV château, our hydroelectric power station, we could walk beside the ponds . . .

Why not?

Indeed, why not? And a few photos for our local bulletin?

Okay, if now.

If now?

You have not the phone?

Oh . . . no.

I have a Sony Ericsson which take photos!

Ericsson-Johansson, long live Sweden!

I am Danish of origin.

Oh. Sorry. Thank you, Madame Rigodin. There now, I'll stand beside Madame Johansson, er, I mean Madame Reynolds . . . could you take the photo, please? Am I in the right place?

Don't you want to put that cup down?

I like the Ricoré what Arthur make.

Say cheese!

Cheese.

Mademoiselle Thiriard!

You wanted me to translate, I'm translating.

There we are. Well, thank you, Scarlett, please forgive us for disturbing you, but we don't see a star here every day, in fact this is the first time we've ever seen a star in our village . . .

In the ass'ole of the world.

Hmm. We had Daniel Guichard in 1975 . . .

I am talking about a real star, Mademoiselle Thiriard, an international star who has won Oscars . . . you understand. Well done, Arthur, you have a beautiful friend there, a very lovely woman, you're a lucky so-and-so, don't translate that, Ginette (said the mayor to Mademoiselle Thiriard). Come and see me at the village hall when you have a moment, Arthur.

And call me at the paper, too, Arthur, here's my card, said Madame Rigodin.

When the three of them had left, Jeanine Foucamprez and Arthur Dreyfuss burst into laughter – a laughter filled with delightful music, the sound of mischievous children, the explosion of joy at the meaningless jokes that cement a happy childhood.

It was fine on that fifth day, and the pleasant weather made Jeanine Foucamprez feel light-hearted; she wanted to go out, go somewhere. Somewhere there's no one else but you, Arthur, and most of all no Scarlett Johansson.

Ten minutes later they were in the courtesy car. Arthur drove south-east, about a hundred kilometres from Long. They listened to the radio; sometimes they sang along to the songs that they knew.

Have you ever compiled a playlist for anyone, Arthur? Jeanine asked.

No.

I'll compile one for you, Arthur, just for you. It will be the playlist of the most beautiful woman in the world, meaning me! And she laughed mischievously.

She wanted to choose the side of happiness, at long last, but in that burst of laughter Arthur Dreyfuss heard a few hoarse notes of grief.

They reached Saint-Saëns (Seine-Maritime) around 11.30, parked the little Honda on the outskirts of the huge state-owned forest of Eawy, and went in.

The air was cooler under the huge beech trees – some of them had trunks over thirty metres high. Arthur and Jeanine stood close to each other, their fingers touching, intertwining, and they walked on like that, hand in hand.

Jeanine Foucamprez looked at him for a long time. In the forest his eyes shone, his awkward body moved more easily, like a dancer's, and she had the impression that he skated over the dead leaves like a water bug on a pond. Here, Arthur's frailties and fears were obscured. Here, *beneath his strong arm / Not even looking at the trees / he doggedly held / all the figures of the world.** It was in this forest that my father disappeared some time after the dog ate Noiya. In the evenings, after school, I used to come back here. I waited for him. He was going to come back; you don't just leave your child like that, not the only child you have left. I waited. I waited here every evening for his sadness *to be lost in the light*, to

* Jean Follain, 'Atlas', *Territoires* (Gallimard, 1953).

fade away *in the sobbing of the wind.*[*] Joy must triumph. Jeanine clung close to him, like a shadow. No, for some sorrows there is no consolation. It's here that I remember him best. He would talk here, murmuring to the tree trunks. He told me about the forest. In the past it was all a huge oak wood, but the wartime bombs scalped and shaved it, and beech trees, which grow faster than oaks, were planted, because human beings are afraid of what is empty and bald, the way it recalls shame and treachery. All our defeats. Although their bodies were warm, Jeanine shivered. Arthur's words moved her; they were unexpected, like magnificent notes being played by a young child on a violin. He taught me about the beech trees, the maples, the sycamores. I preferred the wild cherry trees, they're sometimes called bird cherries. They have such a great need for light that they grow up faster than other trees. Like you did, Jeanine; like I did, too. She shivered. I waited here for my father, looking up into the air. I was sure that he'd climbed a tree, like *The Baron in the Trees*. The what? she asked. It's a book, a little Italian baron aged twelve who decides he wants to live in a tree. They both smiled; they were once more in that early time, the time that Paulham summed up so well in the title

* Jean Follain, 'Tears', *Exister* (Gallimard, 1947).

of one of his stories: *Progress in Love on the Slow Side*. I thought your father was dead, Arthur, that's what I thought. I don't know, Jeanine. Is a person dead when there isn't a body?

Jeanine Foucamprez turned to face Arthur Dreyfuss; her cold hand stroked his handsome face, stroked the warm air coming from his lips, stroked the tiny space between them; they didn't kiss, everything was perfect without kissing; then she put her head on his shoulder; they crossed the impressive avenue of Les Limousins and plunged into the damp shadows of the forest; they walked slowly, swaying a little because of the difference in their heights, but also because it's not easy to be perfectly synchronised at the beginning of a love story. You have to learn to listen not only to the other person's words but to their body, their speed, their strength, their weakness and their disconcerting silences; you have to lose a little of yourself to find it in the other person.

In *Summer of '42*, there is a boy of fifteen called Hermie. The film is set in New England and it's summer. He meets a woman, Dorothy, whose husband has gone off to the war – I'm going to cry, Arthur. The mechanic's arms held her more firmly, *doggedly*. Hermie tries to seduce her although she's twice his age – Jeanine sniffled quietly – and although she's very much in love with her husband. In the end she gets a telegram – oh, here I go – The first tear fell. I'm so silly – a telegram saying that her husband is dead. Arthur's hand gently squeezes hers, his way of saying that he won't interrupt her. And then . . . then she makes love with the boy, and it's so beautiful, so beautiful, Arthur, it's . . . and there's that amazing music, a *lento* with the exact tempo of a beating heart. When dawn comes she's gone, leaving only a few words on a sheet of paper. They will never see each other again. Arthur's hands, surprisingly soft in spite of all the tools and the car engines, wipe away the tears of the most beautiful girl in the world. They are trembling.

Why is happiness always so sad? Arthur asks.

Perhaps because it never lasts.

They head back towards the courtesy car (they haven't met a soul, and Arthur is proud of this fact; she had insisted on a place where there was no Scarlett Johansson). His mobile phone rings and he hesitates to answer it because of the grave and bewitching beauty of the moment, and perhaps because of the proximity of his father, but as no one ever calls him he has a feeling it could be serious. Excuse me please, Jeanine. Hello?

It's the head nurse of the Abbeville hospital.

Your mother has been eating her left forearm, and she's asking to see Elizabeth Taylor.

Autophagia, says the nurse forty-five minutes later when she meets them in the corridor – a hospital corridor, like the ones we all know, neon lighting, green-tinged faces, bad news, and sometimes a smile on an exhausted face, there's a chance of a few more months, a wish to embrace the whole world. The doctor has seen her, he's talking about dementia, we're waiting for the results of some tests but the weight of her brain is already greatly reduced.

Arthur Dreyfuss felt like crying.

He realised that he didn't know his mother, that old woman of forty-six who had eaten her arm, the way a Dobermann had once eaten her daughter. He knew nothing about her. Did she like Mozart, the Beatles, Hugues Aufray? Did she like Swiss wines, wines from

Savoy or Burgundy? Had she any allergies, chickenpox, had she wanted to die of love, to abandon herself to it, had she read *The Baron in the Trees*, seen *Summer of '42*, *La Demoiselle d'Avignon* or *Angélique, Marquise des Anges*? Which actress playing the title roles in those two films would she have wanted to be, Marthe Keller or Michelle Mercier? Had she liked making love, watching aeroplanes crash at the feet of TV presenter Roger Gicquel? Did she love Pierre Lescure, Harry Roselmack, *salade niçoise*, smoked salmon millefeuilles from Chez Picard, *kalb el louz* (a cake made from semolina, almonds and honey), the songs of Michel Sardou, of Jacques Dutronc, and me and me and me, did she love me? As he walked towards the room where she was resting, Arthur Dreyfuss realised that he had already lost her during her lifetime, that he had let her drift away on a tide of tears (and vermouth), that his clumsy, rough and ready attempts at filial love had not filled the void left by the death of Noiya, Beauty of God. He suddenly felt the force of all those years that were lost forever – the words, gestures, affection, all those things that can help avert disaster. Arthur Dreyfuss had waited for his father for years, looking up at the treetops, without noticing that his mother was fading away at his very feet. And now, yes, he began to shed tears: large, heavy tears, like the tears of a child suddenly coming to his senses, although a little earlier that morning Jeanine Foucamprez had whispered to him that nothing ever lasts: a mother, a father, the terrifying sweetness of things.

He hesitated. Jeanine Foucamprez took his hand and led him into the bedroom as if it were a church, their hearts beating faster. Thérèse Dreyfuss, née Lecardonnel, was tied to her bed. Her left arm was swathed in bandages; the nurse said that she would need skin grafts later on, and if they were rejected they would have to amputate part of the arm, give her a prosthesis and rehabilitation. There was a tube up one nostril and another tube coming out of her right arm. The monitoring equipment beside her was making regular sounds, menacing and reassuring at the same time, and on her face, beneath her skin, which was as fragile as lace, there was the laughing mask of death.

I'll leave you alone for a few minutes, said the nurse. If there's any problem at all, just push this bell and someone will come straightaway.

She went out. Jeanine Foucamprez turned to Arthur Dreyfuss. Say something to her, Arthur, she's your mother, she'll hear you, she needs your words like just now in the forest.

I don't have any words to say to her, Jeanine, no words at all. I'm terrified.

So the woman whose rare and comforting body made heads, the whole world, turn, made hearts race, the woman whose body attracted the worst and the best alike, went over to the bed, to the moribund, motionless body, the deliquescent flesh, and her strawberry-red lips opened.

I'm Elizabeth Taylor, Madame. I'm your friend and the friend of your son Arthur as well. Arthur, your son. He's here with me. I've come to tell you that he loves you with all his heart, all his might, but you know as well as I do what boys are like. They daren't say things like that. They think it's not very manly. But I promise you he said this to me: Elizabeth, he said, I must tell you something, I love my mother and I miss her, I understand her pain and her grief, but I don't know what to do, Elizabeth, no one's ever taught me that. I'd like to tell her that I miss Noiya, too, I still hear her laughing in her room, I imagined her growing up and writing pretty poems for Mother's Day, and bringing home a handsome fiancé to meet us one day. I'd like to tell my mother that I cried when Papa left and, like her, I'm still waiting for him to return and if he doesn't come back then it's up to us to find him, to find his tree, you see, Elizabeth, Papa is living in a tree and he's waiting for us there so that we can all be happy, all of us and Noiya, too, she's with him, sitting on a pretty branch where pink flowers the colour of her cheeks grow. We mustn't be sad, that's very important. So that's what your son Arthur told me, Madame – he told me, Elizabeth Taylor, because I love you, too, and I'm terribly sorry not to have known you for longer. Because I've known pain, too, I've known hell. As soon as you're better we can talk about it, we can wait together for those we still miss. Would you like that?

Then it seemed to Arthur Dreyfuss that one finger of the hand weakly attached to his mother's forearm moved, but he couldn't have sworn to it.

Filial love is frightening; its purpose is separation.

They drank a coffee in the hospital cafeteria, in the midst of unhappiness, little girls in shapeless mauve tracksuits, laughing without understanding, fathers on edge because of caffeine, lack of nicotine, and love.

They looked at one another in silence. Arthur Dreyfuss wondered why, in real life, there wasn't music all of a sudden, the way it would happen in a film – music carrying everything away, sentiments, reticence, modesty – and if there had been the music of *Summer of '42* (by Michel Legrand), *Poland* (by Ólafur Arnalds), or a good old Leonard Cohen, for instance, he would have carried her away, here and now in the hospital cafeteria, and he would have dared to say the words, to tell her *I love you*, and she would have taken his hand and kissed him and her eyes would have been shining and she would have whispered, nervously, *Are you sure? Are you sure it's me that you love?* and he would have replied, *Yes, yes, I'm sure, I love you, Elizabeth Taylor, for all that you said to my mother just now. I love you Jeanine Foucamprez for everything you are, for your sweetness, your fears and your beauty. I love you, Jeanine.*

Unfortunately, there isn't a musical score to accompany life as there is in films, only noises, sounds, words, coffee machines going *cling*, the castors on hospital trolleys going *rrr-pfft-rrrr-pffft*, and tears, sometimes cries reminding you that this is all horribly real, particularly in a hospital with deranged patients, emergencies, fear and goodbyes going on forever, and . . . *from time to time there are shadows / a breast revealing / indeterminate pain / a fine, very fine taste of the eternal.*[*]

They looked at each other in silence, and in spite of the absence of music Arthur Dreyfuss took the hand of Jeanine Foucamprez in his own, raised it to his lips and kissed it; he even ventured to put out a few millimetres of his tongue to taste her skin, which was sweet and perfumed, and he found himself imagining what it would be like to lick her all over her body, its

* Jean Follain, 'The Day Labourers', *Exister* (Gallimard, 1947).

mountains, valleys, crevasses and cascades. Jeanine Foucamprez gave a delicious little laugh when his tongue made contact with her hand, but she did not withdraw it, and without actually saying anything, in a place caught somewhere between reality and the ether, far removed from poetry, the two of them tried some words of love.

Excuse me, please, excuse me, aren't you Izzie Stevens?

The apologetic voice belonged to a patient aged about sixty, wearing a dressing gown; she had the simple, dribbling smile of certain children. Aren't you Izzie Stevens? Then you're not dead? Oh, I'm so glad . . .

(To appreciate the incongruity of this response you need to know that Izzie Stevens is a character in the American series *Grey's Anatomy*, played by the actress Katherine Heigl, who was dubbed 'Hollywood's hottest blonde' in 2007 by *Vanity Fair* and whose measurements were said to be a perfect 36-25-36. In any case, in the eyes of a woman of sixty years, twenty of them no doubt spent in front of the hospital TV set, they were comparable to the figure of Scarlett Johansson. In season five of the series, Izzie Stevens, suffering from brain cancer, is left for dead.)

So you're not dead, then?

It took Jeanine Foucamprez several seconds to

understand and then she confirmed that no, she wasn't dead. The woman in the dressing gown let out a terrifying screech: It's not you, that's not your voice, not your voice. You're a ghost! You're dead! And then she scurried away. (It's true that in the French version of *Grey's Anatomy* Katherine Heigl's voice is dubbed by the actress Charlotte Marin and not Jeanine Foucamprez.) Arthur Dreyfuss smiled. Jeanine Foucamprez shrugged her shoulders and pouted: Honestly, Arthur, I've been taken for so many of them – Uma Thurman, Sharon Stone, Farrah Fawcett, especially last year when she died, Catherine Deneuve, Isabelle Carré, even Claire Chazal – and like you with your mother, all I wanted was for someone to come over to me one day and say: Aren't you Jeanine? Jeanine Foucamprez? Oh, you're so beautiful!

Aren't you Jeanine? Jeanine Foucamprez? Oh, you're so beautiful!

Then the beautiful Jeanine Foucamprez smiled a smile that was as lovely as Scarlett Johansson's on the Portuguese poster for *The Nanny Diaries* (*Diario de uma Babá*); she got to her feet, went round the Formica table, and kissed Arthur Dreyfuss on the mouth for the second time. Hidden behind a trolley of hot dishes, the Izzie Stevens groupie, smiling brightly, silently applauded them, delighted. It was an enthusiastic, powerful, electric kiss, a kiss full of life in the midst of pain and fear.

They went back on the road after the doctor had confirmed the diagnosis for Arthur's mother: enlargement of the fluid spaces, loss of Purkinje cells, central pontine myelinolysis, loss of cognitive function and cerebral ageing. Thérèse Dreyfuss, née Lecardonnel, was inexorably diving further into madness, and because Arthur Dreyfuss was trembling the doctor pointed out that nothing could be done, even if his little sister Noiya were to come back that very day, safe and well, nothing would retrieve his mother from the shifting sands that were devouring her, swallowing her whole. So Arthur Dreyfuss told himself that this time he really was an orphan. Even if the poacher's body had never been found, if perhaps there was a chance he had taken flight to another woman's bed, that he lay buried in her plump arms under a large, warm posterior before getting up each dawn; even if his body was rotting away at the bottom of the Condé marsh or was hanging from the highest branch of a beech tree in the forest of Eawy, cheeks torn, eyes dead, his two eyeballs in a crow's beak, facing the sweet valley of the Varenne. Even so, he was an orphan.

They reached Long late in the afternoon on their last day but one.

As they drove past the garage, PP signalled for them to stop. Hello there, lovers, he said laughing (but looking at Arthur), still on holiday? Well, this is all working out nicely. Julie (PP's third wife) suggested we have a barbecue at home this evening, if you'd like, just you two and her sister, who likes the cinema. She could talk to Angelina here, what do you say, Arthur? Arthur Dreyfuss turned to his pretty neighbour, who agreed, amused.

The sister, Valérie, had vaguely wanted to be an actress in the 1990s and had enrolled in drama classes at Theatre 80 in Amiens, a course which offered 'an individual and collective apprenticeship in writing and producing drama', as well as the traditional vocal, respiratory and physical exercises. At the end-of-year show, in front of an audience of thirty-seven, her nerves had left her speechless, so she gave up any notions of Hollywood and found a job as a saleswoman at Nord Textile where her respiratory and physical techniques worked wonders for the lingerie department.

They arrived at 7.30 p.m. PP wasn't there. Julie made his excuses; he had gone to get more wood for the barbecue from the Super U at Flixecourt, she explained, he wouldn't be long. They had brought a bottle of warm L. Benard Pitois champagne, all that they could get from Tonnelier's, and the moment they stepped into the garden the sister, Valérie, exclaimed: That's not Angelina Jolie at all, PP, you hadn't the faintest idea what you were talking about, it's Reese Witherspoon. Oh, my word, isn't she lovely! Oh my God! Do you speak French?

Reese Witherspoon laughed a charming, airy laugh. Yes, Valérie, she said, I speak French and I'm terribly sorry to disappoint you, but I'm not Reese Witherspoon or Angelina Jolie, let alone Scarlett Johansson, even though I know that she and I are as alike as two peas in a pod.

Valérie put down her glass, because she felt this was an important moment, and she was a little ashamed of her mistake.

My name is Jeanine Foucamprez. I'm twenty-six. I

was born in Dury, a few kilometres away from Amiens. It's a village full of flowers, there's a lovely scenic hiking trail, and we have a local horse show. I never knew my father, who was a fireman, because he was burned to death before I was born, trying to save an old lady's life. All he left me was my face. This face. My mother said I was a wonderful baby and then a delightful little girl. The mayor of Dury wanted to hold a Miss Dury competition just for me. That meant I had trouble with my stepfather. He'd have liked to do horrible things to me, the kind that make you want to leave home. Like Jean Seberg in her car. Then my mother didn't think I was pretty any more. She never spoke to me again. I don't know what became of her. I went to live with my aunt. Seven years ago everyone saw my face in *Lost in Translation*. Since the day it came out, on the twenty-ninth of August 2003, I've hated my face. I hate it every moment, every second, of every day. Every time a girl looks at me with contempt, wondering what I have that she doesn't have. Every time a guy eyes me up and I wonder if he's going to approach me, touch me, get out a knife, if he's going to ask for a blow job or just an autograph. Or maybe simply suggest a coffee. Just a cup of coffee. But that never happens. It's not me he's seeing. It's not me he thinks is pretty. It's not me. My body is my prison and I'll never get out of it alive.

For a moment Jeanine Foucamprez lowered her eyes. Valérie wanted to take her in her arms, but she didn't dare. Other people's pain is so hard to deal with. She put out her hand to Arthur Dreyfuss, just as PP turned up again, his eyes shining and with a string bag filled with small pieces of wood in his hand. He saw Arthur go over to the actress, take her hand, and he heard her saying, in a slightly hoarse voice:

Arthur possesses a wonderful gift. He isn't really aware of it, but if anything is broken he knows how to mend it.

Their emotion called for silence. And then, to the sound of the sizzling chops, from which for a good minute or so an alarming and dense black smoke had been rising, PP, who did not understand anything at all about the grace of the moment, tried something – a kind of joke – to bring them back to the soft violence of reality.

Well, hang on, I taught him everything he knows!

Oh, for heaven's sake, you're worse than daft, muttered Julie (his third wife).

Scarlett or Jeanine

They went home on foot in the sobering coolness of the night air.

After that confession – the elegant sadness of Jeanine Foucamprez, formerly known as Reese Witherspoon – they had all turned to other subjects. A little politics, of course: Sarkozy, I just can't think what women see in him, was the opinion of Julie, who was very pretty herself; everything about him is so small, he's a dead loss, apparently the heels and the lifts inside his shoes make him seven centimetres taller. PP, who had started in on the aperitifs, remembered that he'd been nicknamed Naboleon, from *nabot*, meaning dwarf, and anyway in two years' time Strauss-Kahn would see him off, would give him a good seeing to (which seemed like an amusing phrase at the time: that is, before the politician's consenting prick became involved in the scandal of Suite 2806 in the Sofitel, New York; before the cell in Rikers Island jail, then the incident with the girls in the Carlton in Lille, the libertines; before Dodo la Saumure, and the journalist, poor Tristane Banon, and other examples of 'inappropriate behaviour' – the depths to which a human being can sink, the spectacular and miserable fall from grace, the separation). After that, everyone at the barbecue wanted to talk about something other than politicians, those poor fools. Idiots, the lot of them. They were all the same. It was enough to make you vote for Le Pen.

Julie said that Tonnelier's apprentice had seen Christiane Planchard coming out of the Ibis in Abbeville wearing dark glasses and accompanied by a tall, dark, hairy man, which made PP (now on his fifth aperitif) say that if he hadn't been with his wife – and I am with you, Julie, believe me, I am – he wouldn't have minded screwing Planchard on account of the fact there's something a bit crude about her, something . . . he had the word on the tip of his tongue, oh hell, I have it on the tip . . . then Julie pinched his arm with her pointed nails, like the bite of a serpent's fangs. Valérie talked about the cinema (of course, for a former aspiring actress – ah, that's it, cried PP, you've reminded me, it's La Planchard's mouth that's crude, a real treat that would be, wrapped around your . . . another snakebite leaving drops of blood on the biceps of the garage proprietor). Valérie had already seen *Avatar* three times and thought it was an absolute masterpiece, an ab-so-lute masterpiece, greater than France's immortal *La Grande Vadrouille*, the best masterpiece of the last twenty centuries; but that has nothing to do with it, *La Grande Vadrouille*, said her sister; *The Grand Cock-up* if you ask me, exclaimed PP, who was exhibiting the effects of too much alcohol, you can't compare the two morons in that film and the blue people; oh yes I can, because it was the greatest success in the history of French cinema, so it does count, it's a benchmark; stuff your benchmarks, *Avatar* is a global thing, but PP's *Great Cock-up* is typically French. But most of all Valérie couldn't wait for 29 September, when she could go and see *Wall Street 2* with Shia LaBeouf, he's so handsome, the best-looking of all, she confessed, simpering, her cheeks red; all right, I'll admit his name is rubbish – sounds a bit like 'she has the beef'; or *shitting the beef* added PP, and everyone laughed because it was a stupid and coarse remark and sometimes it does you good to be coarse. It reduces distances, erases shame. His beef is about getting nowhere with Megan Fox. Well, it seems that Michael Douglas has throat cancer; oh, I thought it was a tumour on his tongue; in any case

Zeta-Jones will make a mint, see how big she is now, that's for sure, I saw a photo in *Public*, you'd have mistaken her for a pregnant Nana Mouskouri. Anyway, apart from *Zorro*, Zorro? Zozo, yes, babbled PP, what else has she done, what parts has she played, eh? I read that she was bipolar, bi, I'm sure she's bi, slurred PP. Can we talk about something else? This is disgusting! Look, PP, you'd better put more charcoal on unless you want to eat your sausages raw (after charring the cutlets, PP had gone looking for the sausages that his wife had been keeping for the next day). You're a savage! Shitting the beef, though, that's funny, shitting the beef . . . Hilarious, PP, hilarious.

They ate bendy sausages and some burnt potatoes while PP collapsed on the grass. They left him there, like a large steak, for the ants and worms.

Later, they had walked home. The cool night air gently cleared the effects of the alcohol and when Jeanine Foucamprez shivered, Arthur had hugged her.

So now they are in the sitting room, looking at one another. Arthur has put on some music, as you would in a film. Their eyes are shining. They're afraid of going too fast. All their gestures must be perfect, for fear of wounding one another and leaving an indelible scar. She feels moved, her chest is swelling, she's slightly breathless. To Arthur Dreyfuss, it seems as if she is letting a short phrase, perhaps just a word, rise from the pit of her stomach to the surface, allowing it to appear and bloom, bursting like a little bubble in her mouth, a word that will be the key to everything, a word that will forgive everything, the stones with which walls are built, human beauty – but no, it is another word, almost a cruel word, barely stifled by the hand that she suddenly raises to her lips.

Tomorrow.

She stands up, turns as if in slow motion – with regret, it seems. He says nothing, and she disappears into the shadow of the staircase where, under each of her footsteps, the creak of each stair barely covers the thumping of Arthur's heart and his shattered desire.

Alone on the Ektorp sofa, he remembers a saying he had found some years earlier in his fortune cookie in the Mandagon restaurant in Amiens, something along the lines of *It is like waiting for wings. The stronger they are, the longer the journey* (from the Persian Djalal al-din Rumi, 1210–1273). He had thought the saying stupid at the time.

That night, however, he would have liked to know how long the waiting would go on.

On the morning of the sixth and last day of their life together it was raining.

When she came downstairs she was dressed, and he was making the Ricoré. She kissed him on the cheek (oh my God, her scent, my God, those soft lips, my God, her nipple, just brushing his biceps), let's go shopping, Arthur, and buy coffee, real coffee, and she tugged his arm laughing, and if that moment between them may seem banal or stupid to you, imagine it set to music, as it was for Arthur – to Bach's *Orchestral Suite Number 3 in D major*, for instance, with Rudolf Baumgartner on the violin, filmed against a backdrop of rain, her laughter, his own sense of wonder – and you will have before your eyes the image of two shy lovers, a first chance for him, a last chance for her; and later, watching the film again, you will remember that the moment when everything hung in the balance, the moment when they decided to share a life together, or to try to anyway, was when it all began, in that little house on the D32, without words of love, without inane remarks or harlequinades, no, just the moment when they decided to jettison Ricoré in favour of proper coffee.

They went to the Écomarché at Longpré-les-Corps-Saints, where they filled two baskets with coffee, toothpaste (she liked Ultra Brite, he liked Signal), soap (they both agreed on a cream soap), shampoo (hers for tinted hair, his natural), a bottle of oil, pasta (she preferred pappardelle, he liked penne, he bought penne), a jar of jam (she liked strawberry, he liked cherry; she decided, laughing, that they'd buy redcurrant – it's the same colour), toilet paper (she liked the lilac-scented sort, he hated it and preferred unscented, they bought both), green vegetables (I have to watch my figure, she said, laughing, I'm an internationally famous actress), also potatoes (a garage mechanic has to eat well and be strong, and *a potato gratin is absolutely divine*, which was a slogan she'd had to repeat every five minutes in the vegetable section of the Abbeville Intermarché two years earlier), some chocolate (white chocolate for them both; fancy that, he said, something else we have in common), two large coffee cups, one with *Hers* hand-painted on it, one with *His* (and they looked at each other, blushing with emotion, a moving sight, and they held hands all the way to the cheese section), Gruyère, Gouda, Comté that had been aged for eighteen months; they avoided the meat section (no doubt because of Thérèse Dreyfuss, née Lecardonnel, who had been eating her own forearm, and the horrible images that immediately superimposed on a bloody round of beef, steak tartare, or the pinkish bone marrow of veal); they also put a good bottle of wine in the basket (not that either of them knew anything about wine, but another supermarket customer, whose red nose suggested that he was an expert, advised them to buy a Labadie 2007 at €10.90, a Médoc with enchanting notes of red fruit – a little miracle, he said, you can drink it with anything or on its own, I'm thirsty just thinking about it; thank you, monsieur, goodbye), and a large indelible black felt pen (what's that for? asked Jeanine Foucamprez. It's a secret, he replied, a secret), and then they went to the checkout.

Of course the total sum came to much more than Arthur Dreyfuss usually spent when he went shopping and he'd have to be careful until the end of the month. He also thought how lucky he was: some women have to be given jewellery, watches and handbags just to get a smile out of them, whereas Jeanine Foucamprez seemed to be delighted with toothpaste, real coffee, scented toilet paper and one or two bars of white chocolate, all of which gave you a taste for sharing your life with someone else.

On that last day of their life together, which was also really the first, Arthur Dreyfuss discovered one of the simplest and purest forms of happiness: being deeply and inexplicably happy in the company of another person.

Because of the rain they ran back to the courtesy car; Jeanine Foucamprez almost fell on her face, but miraculously recovered (more shared laughter), Arthur Dreyfuss threw her the car keys – you're crazy, she cried, I don't have a driving licence, I failed the test twice. Who cares? he cried; she unlocked the door, trembling, took shelter in the car, laughing all the while as Arthur Dreyfuss put their shopping in the boot, taking no notice of the rain, his clothes as drenched as *a wet floor cloth* – Arthur, you look like *a wet floor cloth*, his mother would have said.

Jeanine Foucamprez thought he looked very handsome as he got into the car, his face dripping with rain, or was it tears of love? You have to put the key in the ignition and turn it to start the car, he whispered, his voice gentle. She smiled, did as he said, and the car started. He put his hand on hers to help her get it into first gear, and no, she didn't stall the engine. She drove the car very carefully for the first few kilometres (at a speed of about 17 kph). Suppose we get stopped? We won't be stopped. She changed into second gear, sighed happily and gently accelerated. I'm not scared with you, she said. The driving test examiner was horrible. He said I wasn't the kind of girl who should be behind the wheel of a car. Turn right, mademoiselle, said Arthur Dreyfuss gently, and don't forget to signal. She laughed and turned into the Avenue des Déportés. And come to a halt at the bus stop. But that's not allowed, monsieur. Everything's allowed, mademoiselle.

Jeanine Foucamprez stopped the car beside the bus stop and Arthur Dreyfuss opened the door, unfolded his tall Ryan-Gosling-only-better-looking form beneath the rain, then took the large indelible black felt pen out of his pocket, and Jeanine Foucamprez watched, amused and intrigued, as he made for the large poster advertising the Dolce & Gabbana perfume The One. She saw him draw a ridiculous moustache and goatee beard, like the one belonging to the Duc de Guise, on the beautiful face of Scarlett Johansson, muse to the famous pair of Italian designers. Arthur threw her a delighted smile, like a naughty boy caught playing a trick, and then covered up the word *One* at the bottom of the poster with an enormous figure 2.

At that Jeanine's heart began beating harder than it had ever beaten before – harder even than on the day when it had been carried away because the little girl had laughed when the light on her bike lit up the world again.

They put their shopping away. Jeanine Foucamprez couldn't refrain from reorganising the cupboards, and the kitchen really needs to be repainted, too, she suggested. I like yellow, it's so sunny. Arthur Dreyfuss let her do as she wanted, even when she threw away three chipped glasses, a casserole dish with something caramelised stuck to the bottom, and a ridiculous tin box with a spaghetti ad on the lid, full of useless items – old French franc coins predating the euro, a plastic spoon, a lucky charm from a Twelfth Night cake, a piece of bark from a wild cherry tree, the message found in a fortune cookie. He left her to settle in and make herself at home, and sighed with delight every time she stretched out her arms to reach above her head, an enchanting gesture that made her breasts more prominent, emphasising their fabulous shape, and deliciously contracting her pale calves – oh my God, so beautiful, how lucky I am, he thought as his heart rose, and a thousand new and at the same time age-old words formed in his mind . . . So, when they had put their shopping away it was time for a coffee – a real coffee, not your horrible Ricoré, Arthur, she said in the same smooth, warm voice as Charlotte (played by Scarlett Johansson) uses in *Lost in Translation* when she tells her husband John: *Mmm, I love Cristal, let's have some*, to which he replies pathetically: *I gotta go . . . and I don't really like champagne* – and the couple in the kitchen that would one day be painted yellow laughed, a gift of pleasure in that moment consecrated only to itself, but they suddenly stopped laughing when they realised that they had forgotten to buy any coffee filters.

At this point Jeanine Foucamprez thanked heaven, and above all Arthur Dreyfuss, for his obstinate preference for natural, unscented toilet paper; think of it, lilac-scented coffee, ugh, what a disgusting idea. And in spite of the tiny pieces of cellulose wadding that floated for a moment in their new *His* and *Hers* coffee cups, before sinking to the bottom like snowy pearls of blotting paper, the large South American coffee beans lived up to the claims of good flavour and body; it was a coffee variety as fruity and light as the Chiapas air where it had ripened, and our two gourmets enjoyed it with their eyes closed, dreaming of the heights of Guatemala, sub-Saharan aridity, a Patagonian lake or the remotest regions of India, parts of the world still without electricity, without television, without the cinema, without the internet, without retail chains, without after-sales service, and without Scarlett Johansson.

Around midday the rain stopped.

They were in Abbeville in less than twenty minutes, less than twenty minutes that Arthur Dreyfuss spent dreaming of driving a convertible with the lovely Scarlett Johansson beside him, her hair blowing in the wind, her cheekbones as shining and smooth and pink as two Pink Lady apples. Jeanine Foucamprez was trailing her hand out of the open window, her hair whipping around in the Honda Civic, and she was wearing a short skirt, the hem of which kept billowing in the wind, revealing the delicious pallor of her thigh. She was enjoying Arthur's confusion while Arthur Dreyfuss drove too fast, concentrating on the road so as to avoid such erotic distractions, so apt to cause accidents.

Your mother has been eating well, a young nurse they hadn't seen before told them, she left her fish but ate all of her potato purée – and the cannibal's son felt a pang as he remembered that his mother had never liked fish ever since she had stopped loving his father, the crooked angler who fished with spoon lures and buzz baits. She'll be a little woozy, she warned them, she's just taken her medication, but she's calmer this morning, although she asked for Elizabeth Taylor twice, which makes me think that she's losing her mind a little, added the nurse, lowering her voice.

She's not losing her mind, replied Jeanine Foucamprez dryly. Her mind is full of wonderful things, she just can't find the right words for them, that's all.

Thérèse Dreyfuss, née Lecardonnel, smiled innocently when she saw Elizabeth Taylor coming into her room.

It seemed to her son that in a single night what little flesh she still had left on her bones had been breathed in and drunk; her skin was so fine that it was no more than a delicate piece of fabric, like Valenciennes lace, and it no longer hid the terrifying angularity of her jaws, her cheekbones and cranial bones; her face was that of a woman who was dead but still smiling, her eyes sunk into their sockets, like two pearls at the bottom of a plughole; her dry and roughened lips were like sandpaper. She articulated, with difficulty: *She came, good, so lovely, angel, dogs don't have wings*, and then the transparent veil of her eyelids covered her lost pearls.

Arthur Dreyfuss and Jeanine Foucamprez each took one of the hands – the left hand was already blue and cold – of the woman who was drowning in the dark and terrifying waters of grief; but the appearance of the breathtaking *Venus in Fur* (starring Elizabeth Taylor) had traced a smile on that striking face that would not leave her again.

Later they went down to the cafeteria, bought two packets of crisps (plain for her, barbecue flavour for him), a Mars bar and a Bounty from the vending machine, as well as two coffees, and while the coffees flowed into the cups drip by drip (not for nothing were they in a hospital), they looked at one another, smiling, and that smile brought their hearts and their fears together and removed them for a moment from all they had lost, all you lose with every step you take: a mother, a memory, a song, a love – all that frightens us, destroys us, dehumanises us.

Love is the only way not to become an assassin.

Thérèse Dreyfuss, née Lecardonnel, that eternal smile now on her face, was dying before their eyes; her soul was going to join Noiya's on the wings of Cleopatra,

Elizabeth Taylor; she wasn't talking or moving any more. A little earlier, in that sad room, Arthur Dreyfuss had tried saying words of farewell and love, because those are often the same thing, but like Arthur himself, the words had taken fright and would not come together properly, so then Jeanine Foucamprez had gone round the bed, sat down behind him, and like a female Cyrano with her black urchin cut and her disturbing curves, her strawberry-red mouth, she had prompted him to say the last words: *I have been happy with you, Maman, thank you. Please tell Noiya when you see her that I love her, that I shall always miss her, she's our Beauty of God*. Arthur Dreyfuss had repeated the words she whispered to him, but tears sometimes drowned a sound, a syllable, a whole word.

I'm not sad, Maman, you'll all be together in the big tree, all three of you, I'll come and see you. And Elizabeth will be there, too, with me, we'll come together, we'll never leave you again . . . I love you, Jeanine Foucamprez had prompted him. Tell her you love her, Arthur. It's so important. That stops a person from dying. *I love you*, Arthur Dreyfuss managed to say, but his mouth was full of salt water, grief, and the immortal words melted away.

The fixed smile seemed to be wavering.

Then Jeanine Foucamprez, overwhelmed, had turned her face towards Arthur's. And thus there would be a cycle of giving. A ripple of eternity. You receive, you give. Arthur had given her a child's laughter, and she had become a survivor, magnificent. In her turn, she was bringing peace to an inconsolable mother, who herself would give all the love in the world to the inhabitants of the wild cherry tree, to the wind, the forests, the dust of which we are made. Love is never lost.

In the cafeteria, the coffee still hadn't finished dripping into the cups.

Suddenly Jeanine Foucamprez put down her packet of crisps, caught Arthur Dreyfuss's hand, trembling, squeezed it as hard as she could and then, in a voice hoarse with fear, put an end to the waiting.

I want to make love with you, Arthur, take me away.

They didn't wait for the doctor on duty, who would certainly have inoculated them with foreign words, *confocal immunocytochemistry*, *round foci in the sub-cortical white matter*, or *cerebral stereotaxy*, which, with a touch of humanity, he would have translated using an understatement: 'Don't worry, it will be all right, everything is going as expected.' No, they didn't want that. They ran to the courtesy car without letting go of each other's hands, as if their blood were mingling through their intertwined fingers. Taking the wheel, Arthur Dreyfuss drove at the crazy speed of an ambulance, transporting a couple seriously injured by love, two victims of grief. They covered the twenty-two kilometres in ten minutes – that is, at an average speed of 132 kph, which was utterly unreasonable, but very wise when you know that in a lightning strike, light moves at 300,000 kilometres per second – that's right, in a single second, and those two had been struck by an almighty force.

They stopped outside the house, the brakes squealing – PP would have something to say about the state of the tyres the next day – and Arthur Dreyfuss kicked the door shut. It slammed like thunder and suddenly, after all that urgency, there was only silence and the paralysis of desire.

They both seemed to be moving in slow motion.

With a graceful movement, Jeanine Foucamprez turned on her heel, her red skirt, like first blood, like the first time, fluttering in the air; her long, pale legs shone for a moment in the darkness of the sitting room, then she leaned gently against the wall, seemed to be posing there, everything about her suddenly seemed so light; her lips, like hallucinations, were shining; her round, high cheekbones were shining; her eyes were shining as they looked at Arthur Dreyfuss, whose mouth was dry, whose hands were moist, whose heart was beating fast. A clear laugh rose from Jeanine Foucamprez's throat, a little aria, the brightness of a pebble dropping gently into the water of a spring, and then, still in slow motion, she flitted over to the stairs, up to the second floor, over to the bedroom and the bed.

When he joined her, she was standing by the little window, her trembling fingers undoing all the buttons of her shirt as you might incise the skin of a fruit to find its heart. Come on, she whispered, come on, it's for you. Arthur Dreyfuss went over to her, reeling slightly. The most beautiful breasts in the world were going to be offered to him. He was going to see them, touch them, caress them, maybe lick them, nibble them, take them right in his mouth; he was going to plunge into them and die, yes, he could die now. He was only a breath away from her, the distance of a kiss away when her dark, satin bra slipped off, liberating the two miracles of the flesh, her perfect breasts, white as an orange surrounded by pith, the areolas light, the nipples hard, so alive. Jeanine Foucamprez was terribly beautiful, her breasts were the most amazing ones Arthur Dreyfuss had ever seen, extraordinary and magical. And *He* and *She*, timid and hot, were beautiful, magnificent in their modesty, still in a childhood that was late to fade away.

Jeanine Foucamprez took the hand of the garage mechanic who looked like Ryan Gosling only-better-looking and put it on her left breast; it seemed to him that her stunning, warm breasts were trembling, but it was his own heart, beating like a drum, panicking, as if a bird were beating its wings in his throat – and when she encouraged her young lover to press harder, to plunge into sweetness, vertigo and pleasure, Arthur Dreyfuss let out a cry, or rather a groan, withdrew his hand quickly and fled into the shadows of the staircase. He had just ejaculated.

We'll pass over any assurances that *it isn't serious, it can happen to anyone*, because for Arthur Dreyfuss it was indeed serious, very serious indeed, and he didn't care about the fact that it could happen to anyone – to hell with that.

It had happened to him.

And he had held the dream of a lifetime in his hand – for six seconds, to be precise, a perfect dream ever since Nadège Lepetit in class three, ever since Liane Le Goff's 36DD cup on the horse in the gym, ever since Mademoiselle Verheirstraeten in middle school, with the furrow between two globes that had made him want a hundred times, a thousand times to be a tear, a drop of perfume, a bead of sweat so that he could lose himself there. He had let that dream of a lifetime get away from him in the most pathetic way possible, in his trousers, in the dark and to his shame, as in those ridiculous hours during adolescence when he had experienced a similar fiasco with a big-breasted girl.

But the soft voice of Jeanine Foucamprez, coming

to his rescue, reached his heart and washed away his shame.

I love it that you want me so much, Arthur. It's really nice.

At that, Arthur Dreyfuss came out of the shadows that were covering him like ashes and rejoined his rescuer on the bed. She was naked and even more beautiful than the millions of photos of a half-clad Scarlett Johansson could leave anyone to imagine. Arthur felt slightly dizzy; over and above that astonishing body, Jeanine was composed of words that moved him deeply, those imponderable little pieces of humanity that go to make up the very weight of things. *Tremors / wind / universe – indeterminate pain / tenderness / dawn.*

And he felt much better about his mishap now, because she gave him a little time before he got a serious erection again, before he plunged into that pale lake, approached its delicately plump banks, that tuft of hair (or *fleece?* – old Mademoiselle Thiriard herself, the amateur interpreter, had hesitated over the right word) – that full, jubilant abundance of hair that she had kept, wild and natural, rather than shaving it, as a tribute, so she said, to the tuft or fleece of Maria Schneider (in Bernardo Bertolucci's famous film of 1972, three years after the first Woodstock Festival where, it is true, the boys had long and rather greasy hair on their heads and the girls had abundant and rather greasy hair in their armpits).

And Jeanine Foucamprez began to laugh, deeply moved by the wondering, childlike and fundamentally simple expression on her lover's face; it was a laugh full of happiness, uncomplicated, laughter that flew high into the air, echoed back from the walls of the room, telling everyone, most of all you, Maman, you see your silence didn't soil me forever after all – and if there had been a song to choose for that moment no doubt it would have been Gainsbourg's *Fuir le bonheur de peur qu'il ne se sauve*, flee from happiness for fear it runs away, and the fragile voice of Jane Birkin, the incredible nostalgia, barely drowning out the wish that Jeanine Foucamprez expressed:

You're not the first person I've made love to, Arthur, but I'd like you to be the last.

Meanwhile Madame Rigodin, the journalist from the *Courrier Picard* (Local News column, Amiens and District) posted a piecc on the Long website.

This post was then tweeted by a certain Claudette, two children who wrote an amateur blog called Walls Have Ears.

The tweet, or phrase containing a maximum of 140 characters, was passed on by Virginie La Chapelle (member of Facebook, fan of Flavie Flament, Dany Boon, Thomas Dutronc and others, also Bruno Guillon according to the photos), who in her turn posted this simple comment on her own wall: 'Scarlett Johansson is in Long, TOTAL BLISS.'

In the following seconds, as well as a hundred or so appreciatively Rabelaisian *likes*, flowery compliments flourished: *Long Island? Where? Long is a hothouse? Scarlett the blonde bombshell – where is she? Seems she's left Ryan Reynolds. In the bay of Ha Long? Long as in my prick? I just loved* The Island. *Great boobs! I ordered the Scarlett Johansson Lifesize Doll, I'll finally be able to screw her.* Etcetera. The height of elegance and chic.

And what with the way friends pass things on to friends and then they pass them on to their friends, a couple of Walloons camping on the site managed by Jipé (he of the punctured tyres) chanced upon Virginie La Chapelle's site. They immediately decided to walk around the little village (9.19 square kilometres) in the hope of bumping into the fabulous actress and then, why not, get a photo of themselves with her, perhaps with the lake of La Grande Hutte – an angler's paradise – in the background. What a surprise for their friends back home in Grâce-Hollogne (a province of Liège, whose inhabitants rejoice in the name of Grâcieux-Hollognois or Gracious Hollognoises).

Meanwhile PP, who liked to surf the Web while his third wife Julie indulged in her weekly beauty routine (removal of unwanted hair, body scrub, face mask, nails, pumice stone applied to the feet, hair tint, then slow masturbation in the warm water from their new five-jet shower head) – PP, then, who liked surfing certain sites he found using keywords such as *saucy*, *hot to trot*, *well-rounded*, and other sites showing one hundred per cent natural beauties, happened naturally and quite by chance upon a site devoted to actresses including Scarlett Johansson. He was upset to discover that Photoshop seemed to have reduced the size of her breasts considerably in the last Mango ads and made a mental note never to buy any Mango fashion products. Well, really, I ask you, he said to himself.

Then, on the same site, he learned that Scarlett Johansson had spent the evening of 14 September at Épernay (Marne department), 150 kilometres from Long (Somme department) where she had arrived the next day. He then had a vision, and shouted to Julie, who had just climaxed beneath the shower head:

Arthur wasn't telling us the truth, my dear! She's not Angelina Jolie, she's Scarlett Johansson!

Arthur Dreyfuss had undressed and was lying beside her.

Their skin shone and their fears had faded. They were holding hands. Arthur didn't yet dare put his own hands on those fabulous breasts. He had tried that already, with results we already know. He wanted to enjoy this long build-up of desire, the time before anything more tumultuous had happened. He wanted to make the most of Scarlett Johansson, to intoxicate himself, fill himself up with the thought of her, enough to last him a lifetime. Perhaps she would leave tomorrow, perhaps she would fade away. But for now, she was here, holding his mechanic's hand, which was dry and strong, like those of his father the poacher, hands that don't let you go, that do not tremble. He was smiling, and he knew, without having to look at her, that she was smiling, too. They began to breathe quickly in time with each other, to the same rhythm; it was music – something delicate, piano music, Keith Jarrett's *Köln Concert*, for instance. The warmth of their linked hands irradiated them, a warmth that combined something of their childhood in it, along with adulthood and the burns it had inflicted.

I'm hot and cold at once, he murmured.

And she repeated: I'm hot and cold at once. Then they both knew that they had begun to make love.

I'm not frightened with you, Arthur. You're gentle. You're beautiful.

He thought of that song by Barbara; he'd loved the words. *Come and let me tell you that / Before you there was no before*. He had forgotten everything else about it except the face of Madame Lelièvremont, to whom he had made love at her pressing request in the back of her Renault Espace – one day when PP wasn't around, of course. Madame Lelièvremont, the notary's wife, had been the one who had really taken his virginity – she was quick about it, vulgar, hungry, exciting, *go on, little one, come, come!* Her urging had excited him, and he had come; there had been an animal howl and he had suddenly loved the impetuous nature of physical love. The shameless side of it. The big-breasted girl in Albert and the notary's wife had been his two first times, but still he whispered in the ear of the beautiful Jeanine Foucamprez: *Before you there was no before* – those were the most beautiful words of love he knew at that moment, and she turned her face gently to his and kissed his cheek. You're so kind. I feel good when I'm with you.

His erection came back and she uttered a charming little laugh – blushing, you might have said. I'm here with you, Arthur, I've chosen you and I don't even know what you like. If you like . . . oh, I don't know. Grilled fish or brochettes. Amélie Nothomb's novels, Céline Dion's songs or, she added, giggling, a *ficelle picarde*. Jeanine Foucamprez turned on her side so that she could see Arthur Dreyfuss properly; her breasts seemed to be sliding, flowing in slow motion, like mercury. It was a lovely sight.

I like reading, he said, but we didn't have many books at home. My father said that when you were reading you weren't living; my mother didn't agree. She borrowed books from the library.

What sort of books?

Delly, Danielle Steel, Karen Dennis, love stories. She said they filled the void that Noiya had left behind, and when she cried she said the words washed away her tears.

That's pretty, said Jeanine Foucamprez.

No, it's dopey.

They laughed.

I once found a book of poetry in a car. A car that had been in an accident. I'd never have thought you could find a book of poetry somewhere like that. That's why I took it. I've read it over and over again. The more I read it, the more I felt that everything a person discovers about life has already been discovered through words, everything you feel has already been felt. Everything that's going to happen is there, in us, already.

Jeanine trembled; he had just understood, not without a certain nostalgia, that words always precede us. I like the words you use, she said.

In one of those poems, he continued, the writer is talking about a young man who has at least half a century ahead of him, and he writes: *He smiles at the banal hope*. Jeanine's face was wistful. It's because of the word *banal*. It's anticipating the end. It tells us that . . .

But Jeanine interrupted him. He didn't take offence. The time for new words would come.

I didn't like poetry very much, she said. I have bad memories of school. Bossuet in the first year of middle school. Someone called Francis Ponge in the next class; he sounded like a sponge. She laughed. But I like Amélie Nothomb. I think she's funny.

I don't know her books.

I'll read you one if you like. And there's Céline Dion, too, you know I like her; she saved me. But I won't mind if you don't like her. Anyway, if you don't like her, then I won't listen to her any more, I promise. (Laughter.) Who's your favourite singer?

Arthur Dreyfuss smiled. I don't have a favourite singer, I like songs, that's all.

Songs like what?

Oh, old songs that PP plays all the time in the garage. Songs from his own age. *Suzanne* by Leonard Cohen, for instance. Reggiani. A song called *Mon vieux*, my old man, by Daniel Guichard; it reminds me of my own old man, my father. It's a cassette that won't rewind properly, so you have to do it with a pencil, but PP loves it because Daniel Guichard himself autographed the cassette for him when he visited the town in 1975. Songs by Balavoine. And Goldman, and Dalida. Peggy Lee, too. A customer left some of her songs at the garage one day.

Jeanine Foucamprez smiled, brought her face close to Arthur Dreyfuss's and kissed him on the mouth. Her tongue was soft and fluttering, like a butterfly's wing, and her eyes were closed. Arthur Dreyfuss's were open, he wanted to see her, look at her; he liked the way her eyes, beneath their lids, moved restlessly from right to left, and sometimes in circles, like the butterfly-wing movement in his mouth. She was concentrating on the moment, she was in love.

Will you take me to the seaside?

Yes.

Which is the nicest bit of seaside?

I don't know, but I went to Cape Gris-Nez once, with PP and Julie.

(For the information of amateur geographers and other interested parties: Cape Gris-Nez is situated between Wissant and Audresselles in the Pas-de-Calais, near a little place called Audinghen, 600 inhabitants, in the middle of the Opal Coast. It's the closest town to England on the French coast, lying exactly 28 kilometres from Dover. Most important of all, ornithologists love it because of all the migratory birds that can be seen there in spring and autumn – buntings, swallows, warblers, skuas and so on. It's a rocky headland with a wonderful view. All the same, sad to say, a lot of people commit suicide there by throwing themselves off the cliffs, with nasty results. After falling forty-five metres the human body looks something like dog food.)

Is it beautiful there?

Yes, very beautiful, because there aren't any houses or cars. I remember thinking that a thousand years ago it must have looked the same, and that was what made it beautiful – time standing still.

I'd love to go there with you, Arthur.

Tomorrow, if you like. I'll take you there tomorrow.

I'm enjoying this moment, said Jeanine Foucamprez. And I'm glad you like the idea of time standing still. I've only ever met the kind of person who's always in a hurry. In year six a boy sent me a poem. I remember it. 'Your Mouth', it was called. I know it by heart. It made me blub the first time I read it. *Your mouth is like a cherry / As red as any berry / I really want to kiss it / I wouldn't like to miss it. / Jeanine, you're such a chick / I wish you'd hold my prick*. Talk about garbage. What an idiot. Idiots, the lot of them. Sometimes I tell myself that I don't have a good body. Because people confuse it with something I'm not. I should have been taller, thinner, flatter, should have had a more elegant body, a less . . . less *exposed* figure (she hesitated on the word *exposed*) and then perhaps they'd have tried to find out what was inside me: my heart, my tastes, my dreams. Like Callas, for instance. If she'd been a real bombshell, they'd have said she didn't sing well, that it was all rigged. But no. With her face, her big nose, her dried-up body, her shadowy eyes, people loved her for her soul and her sorrows.

Jeanine started laughing so as not to reawaken her own.

One day, said Arthur, my father told me it was my

mother's behind that had first caught his attention, the way she had of waggling it behind her like a little chicken. Her bum, the origin of his desire. He couldn't have cared less what she was really like.

And how about you, wasn't it my breasts that first attracted you?

He blushed.

Suppose I'd been ugly as sin? Can there be any desire without the body?

For a few seconds there was no sound but their breathing. *All continued, all was populated by waiting*,* Follain had written. I think there can be desire even without the body, whispered Arthur at last.

For a moment Jeanine closed her eyes and shivered. Then she changed the subject, throwing him a little lifebelt. And since we're talking about what I like, I'd better tell you that I love marzipan and an iced Yule log at Christmas. And I always steal the little plastic dwarves, especially the one holding the saw. And one day I'd like to go to the opera and listen to the music and be moved to tears. Have you ever been to the opera?

No, said Arthur Dreyfuss.

But you'd like to go?

* Jean Follain, *Chef-lieu* (Gallimard, 1950).

Hmm. Don't know.

I once heard the music of *Swan Lake*. It's a lovely story. Very sad. I think the lake is supposed to be made of the tears shed by the parents of a young girl who's been abducted and who turns into a swan at night, and then a prince falls in love with her. His name is Siegfried. It's so beautiful. So . . . tragic. And the music is so moving, it made me cry. It was like a birth.

Arthur Dreyfuss held her close. Neither of them was discomfited by his huge erection. They made themselves comfortable, in each other's arms, she lying on her left side, he on his right, their pale skin merging, reflecting, revealing the map of their desire. They looked at each other, their eyes shining with the future they were tracing for themselves, the music waiting for them, the eternity that such an encounter promises.

I once cried when I was listening to a song, too, said Arthur Dreyfuss. My father had left some time before and my mother kept drinking Martini, waiting for him. I heard Piaf singing on the radio.

Contrary to all expectation, he started singing himself. He had a fine, clear voice. Jeanine Foucamprez was moved. *My God / oh leave him here / a short while yet / the man I love / a day or two or three / or more / the man I saw.* And my mother was dancing in the kitchen, she was naked, holding her glass, she was drunk and the Martini was slopping over the rim, and I thought she looked beautiful in her grief, with her body bare, her little sorrows, she spun round and round like a top, laughing and singing along with Piaf: *Time to love each other / and tell our love / time to make memories*. I looked at her and started crying, then she saw me and beckoned me over to join her. She took me in her arms and made me dance round and round, she fell down and I fell down on her, on her skin, it was cold already. I was crying and she was laughing.

How old were you?

Fourteen.

My darling, murmured Jeanine Foucamprez, lowering her moist eyelids over her sparkling eyes, darling. Arthur Dreyfuss pressed her incredible body to him, her fabulous breasts were crushed against his torso, almost as if he wanted to draw them inside him, to inundate his own chest, as if somehow he wanted to become her, his body to become hers, those breasts, oh, you're squeezing me so tightly, sighed Scarlett Johansson, but I like it, so he hugged her even harder, his penis slipped between her legs and was imprisoned between them, immobilised; he felt the caress of her downy, soft tuft, or fleece, against his stomach, and to take his mind off what was going on lower down, by his balls, he quickly thought of the broken oil container of a Xsara Picasso that he had to change. Don't come now, don't come yet, he thought, but the thighs of Jeanine Foucamprez were rubbing against him, so the broken oil container was followed by the faces of several male politicians, the image of a dog run over on the Chasse-à-Vache road behind the Long campsite, the face of Alice Sapritch in the film *Delusions of Grandeur*, and hallelujah, his eruption was slowly dying down. Don't you like what I'm doing? she whispered. Yes, oh yes, but I don't want to go too fast. You can come, if you want.

He kissed her mouth at length, because he didn't want to talk about the pleasure he was feeling, didn't want to put it all into words; words seemed a little frightening. He had realised that just now, when he was trying to explain the way he'd felt about Follain's book, he had tried to enchant her as he had the day before when he told her about *The Baron in the Trees* in the forest of Eawy, when she had come close to him and they had tried to walk in step with each other.

Perhaps that word was the beginning – silence.

Then Jeanine Foucamprez moved up to the head of the bed so as to offer the mouth of the garage mechanic who was like-Ryan-Gosling-*only-better-looking* her treasure, the breasts that sent billions of men in this world mad: For you, she said, I'm giving them to you, they're yours, all yours – and Arthur Dreyfuss, his mouth dry, kissed that miraculous pair, his tongue tasting every square millimetre of them; his mouth and fingers discovered their milky sweetness, the roughness of the pink nipples hardening between his lips; his cheeks caressed the satiny skin, his nose went down to breathe in new aromas, talc, honey, salt and modesty; Arthur Dreyfuss devoured the breasts of Jeanine Foucamprez, the most beautiful breasts in the world, and he began to cry, and she pressed his handsome face against them, gorged as they were with love, with male desire, like a mother's gesture. I'm here, she whispered, don't cry, don't cry, I'm here.

They stayed like that without moving, intertwined, sealed together, while their hearts found their way back to the calm of tenderness, while the salt on their skin dried; then he murmured thank you, and this made her feel wonderfully happy. I wish we could stay like this for ever, she said, but that's stupid because I know we can't. I wish we could, all the same. He liked hearing her say that, because it was exactly what he was thinking.

That it would be good for something like this never to stop. That you could suddenly converse with tears, because words are too clumsy or too pretentious to describe beauty.

I'd have liked to be an actress, you know. But that's

no good, she added, feigning a happy smile. An actress: can you see my behind in the mirror? No, said Arthur Dreyfuss. In a film, she explained, he would say yes. He would say yes to everything he's asked to do. And how about my thighs, do you like them?

Yes.

And do you like my breasts?

Yes.

Enormously, as the Piccoli character says in *Contempt*. Which do you like best, my breasts or my nipples?

Yes.

Don't be silly, she said, laughing.

I don't know, it amounts to the same thing.

My face?

Yes.

And my heart, Arthur, do you like my heart?

Yes.

And my soul and my fears and my desire for you, do you like all those things?

Yes.

And love, do you believe in love? Do you think I might be the right person for you? Do you think I'm unique, unique in the whole world, rare and precious – that I'm not Scarlett? Do you think you'd love me if I didn't look like this, that I'd have my chance, like every other woman in the world?

Yes, yes, yes and yes. You're Jeanine Isabelle Marie Foucamprez, and you are unique, and these last few days spent with you I've been discovering the beauty of things, of taking it slowly, now *It's enough to touch the bolts and gratings / To feel the ineluctable weight of the world.** I can be afraid because maybe fear is a form of love (Jeanine's forefinger caressed his lips and he shuddered), and I love your fears, all your fears. We both have pieces of us missing, Jeanine. How can I put it? You don't have a body that's all your own, and I don't have the body of my father who may have loved me but never said so. It's the same for both of us. We're the same kind.

We're both slightly dented.

Jeanine Foucamprez buried her face in the pillow for a moment, not wanting him to see her reddened eyes. Do you think we can be repaired? Do you believe in God? In fate? Do you think forgiveness is possible?

Yes, said Arthur, then he corrected himself: No, in fact no, I don't think so. I can't forgive my father, considering that I won't ever see him again.

So you'll always be dented.

And how about you? Have you forgiven your mother?

* Jean Follain, 'Junk Jewellery' (or ironmongery), *Usage de temps* (Gallimard, 1943).

Jeanine Foucamprez smiled. Yes. I forgave her the night I decided to come here. When I chose not to end it.

How about the photographer?

He wasn't the one who hurt me. He was doing his dirty job, being a man, that's all; he didn't hurt me. It was her silence, that was what hurt. The fact that she wouldn't touch me. Being nothing but a piece of shit to her, that was what hurt the most. Back then, I'd have loved God to exist. With his little paradise, his cotton-wool clouds where you find the people you love again. Where you can't be hurt any more. Do you think my father would have recognised me?

I don't know, sighed Arthur Dreyfuss.

Do you think he would have taken the dents out of me?

He put out his hand, placed it on her breasts and slowly caressed them. He wasn't afraid of doing that any more. He looked at them, he looked at his hand, his fingers, he felt the weight of her, brushed her silky skin. He thought: these are my fingers, this is my forefinger, that's my blood, that's my thumb touching the breasts of Scarlett Johansson, well, of Jeanine Foucamprez, it's almost the same thing, because neither Josh Hartnett nor Justin Timberlake nor Jared Leto nor Benicio de Toro has ever touched these. *Before you, there wasn't any before*. And the more he caressed them, the more Jeanine

Foucamprez arched her back, her mouth slowly went dry, her sighs became hoarse, her skin was covered with tiny drops of water; sometimes her eyes seemed to roll right up, and Arthur Dreyfuss could see only the whites, two milky eyes, which scared him slightly, but he knew, since that time with Madame Lelièvrement, that a woman's pleasure – the wave, she'd called it, it's a wave, little one, a wave breaking – could set off surprising reactions, from the sweetest to the most alarming.

Jeanine Foucamprez's breasts were amazingly erogenous. Arthur Dreyfuss thought proudly that her orgasm was being born from the touch of his own fingers.

When, with a cry, the fabulous body suddenly contracted and then, with a groan, relaxed entirely, Jeanine Foucamprez went all red, her forehead feverish; he thought she might be ill, but she smiled, reborn, and put her burning hand on her benefactor's cheek: Hold me, please, and Arthur Dreyfuss, overcome by her words, was unable to do anything else.

When the wave had retreated entirely the 'most beautiful woman in the world' opened her luscious mouth, opened her full, shining lips, and out of them – gracious, airy, and all-embracing – came the remark that no man on earth would not have dreamed of hearing:

You can penetrate me now if you like.

Arthur Dreyfuss did not jump at the chance – even if he would have quite liked to have ejaculated at that moment – and the words coming out of his attractive mouth were his very own now; he realised as he was saying them, words of love, simple, sincere, definitive, as when you give yourself body and soul for the first time: I have to tell you something, Jeanine. Before I met you, I had a dream. An Audi garage, a big concession in Amiens or anywhere else if the chance arose – Long is too small, there's only the mayor and the notary and maybe Tonnelier who could afford an Audi – a fine garage, a clean waiting room with leather armchairs and a Nespresso coffee machine, new magazines every week, not old things like PP has with their corners all damp and dog-eared, with the crosswords already filled in and the cookery pages torn out; but I tell you what, you've made that dream fly away. Jeanine sat up. Arthur smiled soothingly. It's given way to something better. Which doesn't frighten me any more. I'd like to go back to studying. I want to learn how to use words. Learn to find the right words, arrange them so that I can cast a spell on things. Like music. His strength of feeling made Jeanine shiver. But I'll go on working for PP so that we have enough money to live on, don't worry, I'm not going to let you down.

I'm not worried, Arthur. Jeanine Foucamprez was trembling; she knew that that was the finest declaration of love that a twenty-year-old garage mechanic could make. She pulled the sheet up over their burning bodies because suddenly she felt cold. She buried her beautiful face in the mechanic's shoulder and her mouth the colour of strawberries murmured *yes* into his ear, *yes*, Arthur, I'd like words to be your tools, *yes*, I'd like you always to caress my breasts the way you did just now, and *yes*, I want to see Cape Gris-Nez with you and stop people falling over the edge and turning into something horrible like dog food; *yes*, I'd like to help your mother and look after her, and be Elizabeth Taylor if that's what she wants; *yes*, I'll learn to like Signal toothpaste and penne and natural unscented toilet paper, and all the things you like, everything you like, and *yes*, I'll forget all the songs by Céline Dion and learn songs by Édith Piaf and Reggiani, Arthur, and *yes*, *yes*, *yes*, I'd like you to make love to me now, please make love to me all the way to my heart.

Dusk was falling. The shadows outside were swallowing everything: animals and humans, and all their sins.

In the only bedroom on the second floor of Arthur Dreyfuss's little house, the intertwined bodies had the elegant pallor of a picture by the Danish artist Vilhelm Hammershøi (1864–1916; whose interiors are rendered with an ethereal grace, a magnetic light, and which certainly represent the finest definition of the word 'melancholic', for that was what they are all about, *melancholy*.)

Arthur Dreyfuss and Jeanine Foucamprez had suddenly discovered love.

There was nothing sexual in their movements now; it was more like Tchaikovsky's ballet that had made her cry when she dreamed of Prince Siegfried – and if Arthur Dreyfuss was making love to her now, as she had wanted, yes, he had also managed to touch her heart.

The two of them, clumsy and graceful at the same time, were relishing each new second, each tormented and fascinated second, because already it would be the last.

Every first time is a crime.

They looked at each other in the shadows. Their eyes were shining, and talking, saying things that need no words. They marvelled at their own beauty. Their fragility terrified them. What they were losing was killing them – but that was the violence of things. That was all there was to it.

Jeanine Foucamprez was beginning to gasp, the heart of Arthur Dreyfuss was swelling; tears mingled with their sweat, the scent of their bodies was sweeter now, headier, a bitter sap, vulgar and delicious; she groaned, he cried out; they wept – *the wave, it's a wave, little one*, the notary's impetuous wife had sung out; the wave was sweeping everything away, tearing and crushing everything, their entrails, their last defences; then their bodies shook and took flight, knocked against the bedroom walls; they laughed, denuded, stripped bare, streaked with blood, they feared nothing any more, they could lose themselves now and die; it was done, and all the rest would be only memory, the impossible road to come back here, to the first, unique time.

Melancholy.

When their bodies fell back on to the drenched bed, when its dampness made them shiver and the salty chill began to make their fingers go numb, Arthur Dreyfuss sighed, gently intoxicated, in love, and words that could change a life left his mouth.

I love you, Scarlett.

And Jeanine's heart stopped beating.

Arthur Dreyfuss was sleeping, his face peaceful as it rested on the prodigious chest. There was a child-like smile on his mouth. Jeanine Foucamprez stroked his hair, his forehead, his soft skin; she was not sleeping.

It seemed to her that she would never sleep again. She was not crying. Her tears had been shed earlier in the night, floods of tears, a short while after her lover had fallen asleep, after his head had grown heavy on her breasts, and her tears had carried away all her dreams. She had none left now.

I love you, Scarlett.

Day was dawning outside, over towards Condé-Folie, beyond the marshes; there were few clouds, no wind. It was going to be a fine day, calm weather like those rare mornings when Louis-Ferdinand Dreyfuss used to take his son to the Croupes pond or the Planques river to go fishing – one of their silent, men-only moments. Jeanine Foucamprez was smiling sadly. She had forgotten to ask if he liked animals . . . Because I would have liked to have a little Brittany spaniel one day. Spaniels are good dogs, you know. Intelligent, lively, docile. They are good with children, too, and I'd have liked to have children one day, too. Would you have liked that, Arthur? I can imagine you with a daughter, a little girl called Louise, that's a pretty first name. It was my grandmother's name. I remember her, even though she died when I was only six. She smelled of mothballs; it was funny. One day I asked her what her perfume was called, and she said it was wardrobe perfume, imagine that, *wardrobe perfume*. Whenever I went to see her she took one of her pretty dresses out of the wardrobe, wearing it just for me so that I'd think she looked beautiful. But you're pretty anyway, Granny, I said. And she said no, no, but as for you, you're going to be the prettiest girl in the world, and I laughed and said oh, you just say anything that comes into your head, Granny, and she would reply, with her mouth all twisted, don't laugh, Jeanine, being the most beautiful girl in the world is the worst thing that could happen to you.

Suddenly Jeanine Foucamprez closed her eyes and murmured, as if to herself: Yes, I know, Granny.

You make people unhappy.

She opened her eyes again. And then I saw you, Arthur, with that little girl, and I wanted you to look at me the way you looked at her, and you've given me that look every minute, every second of these last six days, and I really do thank you for that. Because for the first time in my life I felt I was *me*. I felt happy and alive and so clean in your eyes. So clean. Everything was simple, everything was going to be so simple at last. But now it is so painful. I feel so sad.

I'm Jeanine, Arthur, not Scarlett.

Very carefully she raised her lover's head with one hand, slipped a pillow under it with the other; she left the bed where melancholy lay and went down to the kitchen without a sound, avoiding the tricky steps on the staircase. She went into the kitchen that was going to be painted yellow one day.

She took the keys of the courtesy car from the table and left.

Outside, the cold air clawed at her.

She got behind the wheel of the Honda Civic, thought for a moment of the driving test examiner who had once let her know that the right place for her was in the passenger seat – she hadn't understood his insult at the time. She started the engine. The memory of Arthur Dreyfuss's hand on hers when she put the car into first gear made her shiver.

There was no one else driving along the narrow D32. She left Ailly-le-Haut-Clocher behind her, drove down into Long, towards the heart of the village, PP's garage, the Grand Pré campsite.

Suddenly she felt the calm that immense grief can bring.

She accelerated; she wasn't frightened any more.

Third gear, fourth gear. She passed À la Potence and Au Buquet at over 90 kph. She was laughing. It felt as if the car were flying. Her body felt so light, she was almost happy. There were the first houses in the distance. Beyond them, the marshes where Arthur had grown up surrounded by silence. She smiled, imagined him fitting the hooks with bait for those illicit nights of carp fishing with his mute father, those nights long ago as he grew up to be a man, a journey that would one day bring him to her – all those nights now lost. The steering wheel shook in her hands. The needle of the speedometer was at 115 kph. The tiny chapel of Our Lady of Lourdes lay ahead; it was situated at the place where the D32 and the road to La Cavée, which went steeply downhill, met in a Y shape. They had passed it on the third evening of their life together; she had felt cold, he hadn't yet dared to take her in his arms and warm her, he hadn't dared to risk the words of a man, words jostling each other, taking without asking, ravishing . . .

She would have said yes that evening. All those evenings, all those days she would have said yes.

Yes, Arthur.

The little chapel suddenly appeared. She accelerated again. The car crashed into the narrow blue door of the oratory at nearly 120 kph, as if it wanted to pass through into the chapel. Yes, Arthur, I tell you, yes. The brick walls stood up to the impact, the car stopped instantly. Inside, the body of Jeanine Foucamprez was thrown forward, the airbag was not released, her lovely face was smashed against the windscreen, which broke, and her face passed through it; sharp blades of broken glass lacerated her pink skin, tore an eye, an ear, carved into her strawberry lips, and suddenly everything was crimson and sticky, a terrible red; her magnificent breasts exploded against the steering wheel, her ribs were crushed into small pieces, and her compressed, choked heart went on beating gently; her legs were crushed by the engine as it thrust through under the dashboard, with a dreadful, barely audible sound of breaking bone – and suddenly the scene was a Francis Bacon painting, an amaranthine pulp. The pain was so inhuman that Jeanine Foucamprez did not feel hurt, or else she had no words for such terror; she vomited up her heart, she vomited up her soul.

It took her long minutes to die, and when at last she suffocated, amid that ugly scene, she was still crying.

I'm Jeanine, Arthur, not Scarlett.

Arthur Dreyfuss woke up feeling happy. His hand felt for the body of Jeanine Foucamprez and its warmth. The bed was cold

There was no sound in the house. No sound outside it, either.

At this early hour only the bakery in Ailly-le-Haut-Clocher (4.5 kilometres away on the D32) was open, and on very windy days the aroma of croissants, milk rolls and other varieties of brioche glazed with brown sugar would scent the air, wafting in under the doors of houses and making people still asleep smile as their mouths watered.

Arthur Dreyfuss leaped out of bed. *Jeanine?* He imagined her downstairs, in the kitchen that would be yellow some day. He smiled. She's making coffee, he thought, using large South American coffee beans grown in Chiapas. He wants to join her, take her in his arms, say thank you to her, tell her I love you, Jeanine, make love to her again, and drink the sweet, full-bodied coffee with her. He wants to ask her if she likes animals, he wouldn't mind having a little dog one day, to accompany him when he goes fishing, some kind of spaniel; he will teach her how to use all kinds of fishing tackle, he will pass on to her the knowledge he inherited from his father, the poacher whose body has never been found. He finishes dressing and goes downstairs. *Jeanine?* He thinks that he is the happiest man in the world. He tells himself that they will go and see his mother at the hospital, he and Elizabeth Taylor. He will find the right words this time. Maman, this is the woman I want; with Jeanine, I'll be able to stay alive. I'll be able to find the words I lack. To allow Papa to fly away, let him go. We'll never mention Scarlett again. He runs down the creaking stairs. They'll go and see the librarian as well. She will tell him this 'friend' is actually love. Above all, don't slip, don't fall, don't hurt your head. Just go up to her in the kitchen without scaring her and hold her tight. But there is no sound, no smell of coffee; only silence when he reaches the landing. *Jeanine?* He goes on down, avoiding step number eight that squeaks like a mouse: he mustn't wake her if she's dropped off to sleep again on the sofa. But she isn't there. She must have gone out to get bread and croissants. He smiles. She is beautiful. He misses her already. He shivers. He gets out the coffee, a pan for the water. He will read her Follain's poems. *You see a wisp of smoke / a leaf flying away / only man is obliged to sense the passing day.*[*] From now on, he will let the words grow in him, and she can pluck them. He knows that words are a field, and the order in which the wind arranges them can change the world.

The coffee is ready.

The air in the kitchen is sweet and feminine. He would like her to be there now. Time seems to drag without her. He wants to begin their life together. He wants to go back to the little chapel of Our Lady of Lourdes. He will venture gentle force this time. Here she is, knocking on the door. He runs to open it and sees PP before him. An unrecognisable, unhappy, wretched PP, his eyes bloodshot, bright; his blackened hands are shaking and tears suddenly fall from his eyes; his dry lips are sticking together, as if they have been sewn up, holding back the words that will end everything, will end the world. Arthur Dreyfuss is going to howl out loud. PP takes him in his arms, holds him to stifle his pain, absorbs Arthur into himself.

* Jean Follain, 'Absence', *Territoires* (Gallimard, 1953).

Arthur

It's a fine day. The garden is still green. Jeanine Foucamprez is sitting at the table; there's a plate of fruit on it and two glasses of wine. She is very blonde. She is wearing a thick, dark brown cotton blouse with a heart-shaped neckline that reveals the top of her fabulous breasts. Beside her is Javier Bardem, his clothes covered with splashes of oil paint, offering her a coffee. He spills a little and apologises; she smiles, it doesn't matter, no, no thank you, no sugar. Jeanine Foucamprez doesn't take sugar in her coffee. They make a handsome couple. On the other side of the table, her eyes black, her hair black, her soul black, Penelope Cruz is watching them and smoking. Her left forefinger is massaging her left temple. The tension between the three of them is perceptible. So is the desire and fascination. Then

Javier Bardem suggests a walk in the country, and Penelope Cruz turns down the idea with a scathing: It's definitely going to rain. She speaks to Javier Bardem in Spanish and Jeanine Foucamprez doesn't understand. She is slightly humiliated, she is wounded, so Javier Bardem tells Penelope Cruz to speak English. Didn't you ever learn to speak Spanish, she asks Jeanine Foucamprez. No, Chinese, I thought it sounded pretty. Say something in Chinese. *Hi ha ma* (at least, that's what it sounded like to Arthur Dreyfuss; Chinese is difficult to transcribe). You think that sounds pretty? Penelope Cruz asks cruelly. Jeanine Foucamprez seems to sag; she would like to get out of this situation, run for it, go far away, probably, far away from the drama, the storm that's brewing. But Penelope Cruz rises to her feet first, lights another cigarette, and Javier Bardem does the same. They are both painters, theirs is a physical, violent form of painting, a bond between them, indestructible, impossible, and Jeanine Foucamprez senses that, knows that she will not be able to resist their darkness, their ghosts, their desire for dead bodies, for sex, for redemption and loss. There they go, shouting at each other. He stole everything from me! cries Penelope Cruz. Javier Bardem defends himself, I'm not saying you were not influential but . . . and their voices are rising. They could have killed each other one day, a chair thrown, the slash of a razor; it was jealousy, the Spanish woman shouts, you betrayed me with your eyes, with Agostino's wife, and Javier Bardem shouts back, and Jeanine Foucamprez, lost between the two of them, suddenly looks so frail that tears come to Arthur Dreyfuss's eyes; he would like to burst into that garden, tell them to shut up, *callaos, callaos!* then take Jeanine in his arms and hold her tight until their hearts are beating in time with each other as they did before, as they did before.

But in *Vicky Cristina Barcelona* you can't get into or out of the film, as you can in *The Purple Rose of Cairo*, so he presses Pause.

And the dark loneliness swallows him up.

When the police had arrived at the scene, they had called PP because of the sticker saying *Payen Service Station, Courtesy Car* on the rear window of the crushed Honda, and because the firemen hadn't found any clue as to the identity of the dead woman inside.

One of them thought she had beautiful hair, and shed tears.

Then traffic on the small D road built up all the way back to La Potence. Then people began to arrive, walking heavily, as if going to Mass. There was Christiane Planchard and her shampoo girl and the colourist, walking arm in arm with each other, pale-faced; Gabriel Népile, the mayor; Mademoiselle Thiriard (wearing a curious bright red, almost fluorescent cap of the

Phrygian kind that hid her massacred fringe); Madame Rigodin, the local journalist (without make-up, a terrifying but curiously more human sight); Éloïse from Dédé's chip shop and the sturdy truck driver whose first name was probably Philippe, in view of the new tattoo on the waitress's wrist; there was Valérie, once an aspiring actress (her cheeks scored with folds still warm from her pillowcase), and Julie, a devotee of the shower head with five jets, also PP's third wife; there was Madame Lelièvremont in her flesh-coloured slip with the scooped neckline that sometimes revealed her pathetic breasts, the mules she wore as bedroom slippers on her feet, a scarf tied around her rollers and suddenly looking as if she were a hundred years old; there were those two Belgians, dressed in their Sunday best for the photo they had dreamed of having taken with the American actress, a couple whom no one noticed or heard and who understood nothing of what was going on, but who took pictures of the chaos, the grief and tears of others at the scene. The Belgian couple were asking whether it really was the famous Scarlett Johansson, the American actress, if this was a scene from the film, a stunt, this accident, special effects, it was incredibly realistic, and where was the camera, and who was the young actor in tears, he was screaming now, and people were preventing him from getting any closer to the flattened car, from plunging into the pools of blood mingled with oil on the ground in distorting shadows? Who was that boy saying he wanted to die, die, die, imprisoned in the enormous, dirty paws of the garage proprietor who was uncannily like Gene Hackman? The local priest was there; Tonnelier from the butcher's and charcuterie, who had brought coffee and small snacks: tuna fritters, Emmental cheese straws, broad-bean bites, breadsticks with olives and parsley pesto (these titbits had been ordered for a wedding at the château later that day, but never mind that, the culinary artist had spluttered, who cares? It's when calamity strikes that you need food, not when you are happy); and later in the morning the librarian aunt and her postman husband arrived, their eyes exploding with tears, their grief disfiguring, and there had been more cries and tears, grief, and boundless fear.

The young star driving alone
has overturned taking a bend
full of sky
and beside her groaning engine
*a toad dies with her.**

* Jean Follain, 'Landscape with Young Star Dying', *Usage du temps* (Gallimard, 1943).

Later, after *Vicky Cristina Barcelona*, he will watch her films in order. He will see her growing up. He will see her growing old. Her films will be their photo albums.

He will never leave her again.

He will follow the film by the New York clarinettist with Frank Miller's *The Spirit* (2008), in which Jeanine Foucamprez plays the part of the *femme fatale*, Silken Floss, the secretary and accomplice of Octopus. Then, when he has watched that one ten times, a hundred times, when he has had his fill of it, he will watch *He's Just Not That Into You*, directed by Ken Kwapis (2009), in which Jeanine Foucamprez plays the part of Anna, a pretty blonde (as usual) who flirts with Bradley Cooper.

He will watch her again at the age when she came to

ring his doorbell one evening – when he was wearing his Smurfs undershirt and boxer shorts – as an incendiary redhead, dressed in a matt black skintight jumpsuit, as Natasha Romanoff, alias the Black Widow in *Iron Man 2*, made by Jon Faveau.

And while he is waiting for Cameron Crowe's *We Bought a Zoo*, starring Jeanine Foucamprez and Matt Damon, or Joss Sheldon's *Avengers*, in which she resumes the role of the Black Widow, not to mention *Hitchcock*, directed by Sacha Gervasi, in which Jeanine will play Janet Leigh, Arthur Dreyfuss listens to her records in a continuous loop: *Anywhere I Lay My Head* (after the songs of Tom Waits) and *Break Up*, recorded as a collaboration with Peter Yorn.

And while he waits, he continues shedding tears.

He has put his house up for sale, and even if the young guy from the estate agent doesn't seem too optimistic: it's the credit crunch, you see, it's all going to blow up in our faces, it's a bubble, speculation, people are going under, and yours is such a small house, I couldn't imagine a young family in it, unless they're a family of dwarves, ha, ha . . . oh, sorry, I do apologise, that's not funny. Still less a young couple, given what happened, hmm, well, I didn't mean to say that, but . . . but Arthur Dreyfuss believes he did: to hell with the price, I just want some money, I want to get out of here, understand? I understand, I'm doing my best, monsieur, but it's not easy.

Several months later, when the house was finally sold (at one third of the asking price, but too bad), Arthur Dreyfuss went to the hospital in Abbeville for the last time.

Thérèse Dreyfuss, née Lecardonnel, had fallen into a coma a short while after their last visit, following generalised seizures, the doctor explained. She is in a deep coma, meaning that she doesn't react to painful stimuli and her electroencephalogram displays delta waves that don't react to any external stimuli. She's in the final stages. What do you mean, the final stages? Arthur Dreyfuss asked. The end, young man, it's the end. She's here, but not really here any more.

Her eyelids looked as if they were made of dust. Her mangled arm had finally had to be amputated because of a nosocomial infection and Arthur Dreyfuss told himself that now she would never be able to take him in her arms again, any more than she could hug their little Beauty of God, if the two of them were ever reunited.

The doctor went off. Push this button if you need anything, I won't be far away, and Arthur Dreyfuss shrugged his shoulders: yes, I do need something, I need her; I need you, Maman, I need Papa and Noiya and Jeanine. He smiled sadly when he said her first name. He had never said it since the accident. Jeanine. It was Elizabeth Taylor, Maman, you liked her because she was beautiful. Because she made you forget about dogs for a moment. He takes her remaining hand in his; it is freezing. The cold makes him shiver. You weren't afraid any more with her. You were smiling. He sits down. He looks at the empty body that bore him. Brought him forth. He can't imagine how a man could have come out of such a slight body. Such a shadow. Because from now on she is a shadow and he is a man. He knows that. There are acts of violence and of grace that upset the natural order of things and make you grow old. That lifetime of six days he'd had with Jeanine Foucamprez has changed his world as much as a war, the sort that ends badly. That changes the survivors, tipping them over into madness. Or into the immense tenderness of humankind.

She's gone, Maman, very far away. She's gone to America. He tells her that Jeanine dreamed of becoming an actress. He tells her that she performed the famous scene from a film starring Brigitte Bardot for his benefit. Brigitte Bardot and Michel Piccoli. He tells her some of the amusing dialogue. He smiles, but melancholy is never far away. He utters new words, new arrangements of words, and lays them at his mother's feet, a coat of words that he uses to make things easier. *They wanted to take her flesh / She wanted to give her heart*. The flowers that Jeanine was to pick are growing. *I loved her truth / Her frail fragility / In the deepest part of us / The colour of her soul. I think of her soul / lying to herself / unloved*. She wanted me to see her through her own eyes, Maman. She showed me her heart. It was wonderful and sad. I think there's something almost beautiful about sadness.

He lets the words flow from him, a gentle river carrying away absence, pain and childhood. He listens to them; he understands that you are never loved for yourself but for the gap you fill in the other person. You are what is missing in other people. Jeanine had been abandoned by her mother after those photographs. Arthur had been abandoned by his father, for no reason known to him, one day when he went poaching. He knows that you can die from being punished for no reason, even when you don't have anything to blame yourself for. You are lost. In choosing to sink, his mother had also abandoned them all. He looks at her now. He finds her fixed smile both distressing and ugly. He remembers her kisses when Noiya was alive. After that, nothing. Her mouth never kissed anyone again. It just bit them. His hand can bring no warmth to his mother's. Perhaps she is already dead, even if the machinery is still making little noises. Machines don't know everything. They sometimes lie. *I loved her beauty / In the absence of her body*. I miss her, Maman. She was the only living person I had left. We were saving each other. He repeats that Jeanine is far away. In America now, because it's difficult for actresses here these days. Even if you are someone. Even if you're sublime. If you have the type of body that would inspire a painter. Like the Botticelli painting you liked on that stamp. Even if you arouse the primal desire of men, all men. And while the cold begins to numb his own hand he announces that he is going away, that he has sold his house. He left his job with PP last week because he is leaving on Monday. This coming Monday. He is taking a plane from Paris-Charles de Gaulle airport. But it will be all right. He's not entirely sure of that. He's been told there are tablets you can take to help with the fear of falling, the fear of finding yourself without wings, the fear of infinity. It will be the first time he has flown. He has asked for a window seat. Then he will be able to see them in the wild cherry tree, Noiya and their father. They'll wave at each other. They'll blow kisses. And they'll be a family again. He wonders if his mother's soul has already joined them in the tree. He thinks it has. He thinks that you always go back to the place where you sinned. He gently lets go of her icy hand. It's a first goodbye. He smiles. I know that America is a huge place, very large, fourteen times bigger than France, I read that somewhere. But I'll find her.

He supposes she is in New York or Los Angeles. You don't make a career by sitting about quietly in Caroosa (Oklahoma). He has found the address of her agent on the internet; his name is Scott Lambert. He even has his telephone number. I'll find her because I love her, Maman. I want to spend the rest of my life with her. And have a little girl, and some kind of spaniel, go fishing together and then go back to college, or make some other dream come true for the two of us. Three of us with the little girl. Without her, nothing is very good. Since she went to America he's been having stomach pains again: you know, like when Papa left us; I have pimples that get infected, so I'm not very well right now. I'm not sleeping too well, either. He thinks of the bad things you can sometimes do without meaning to. He knows now that loving someone can kill them. That's terrifying. His first words as a murderer. A phrase by Follain comes back to him. *At insidious moments villages, rivers, valleys lose their meaning / The bird, the leaf both tremble to exist.** He guessed long ago that Follain's words were talking about fear and loss. Talking about him, his very existence in the balance.

I know that she isn't Jeanine, Maman. He will explain when he's found her. He will tell her everything and she will understand, he's sure of that. He has learned some English sentences off by heart. *I'm a garage mechanic, do you have a job for me?* And: *You resemble someone I prodigiously, prodigiously loved.* Prodigiously. He likes that word. He feels there's something divine about it. I'd like to find that place of love again, he will explain. He'll tell her all about it. Their meeting, their story, shopping at the Écomarché, the coffee filtered through toilet paper. I'll tell her about the first time we laughed ourselves silly, and that it was over a porn DVD – also the only time he lied to her by pretending it wasn't his. I'll tell her the story of *The Baron in the Trees*, and *Summer of '42*, and how I took her to the hairdresser to get rid of her ghosts, how she was Elizabeth Taylor for you and Cyrano de Bergerac for me, how she taught me to tell you I love you, even if it's difficult, even if tears sometimes make the words melt, dissolve whole syllables;

* Jean Follain, *Tout instant* (Gallimard, 1957).

I'll tell her how we loved the same things at the same moment, and how we started to fly when we made love; we flew like birds, Maman, and she will understand. Did you fly with Papa? Yes, she will understand. He even told his mother so in English. And everything will be back in its proper place. If not, I'll die, Maman, I'll die. No one can live like this. She has lost her daughter. She's losing her son. I know that perhaps she won't want me to call her Jeanine, but never mind. I'll call her Scarlett if she'd prefer that. She has lost them both.

It's over. The machine isn't making any more sounds. Yes, I'll call her Scarlett if she'd prefer . . .

Scarlett

Scarlett Johansson was sitting in the back.

She was talking on the telephone to Scott Lambert, her agent, about the possibility of playing Marilyn Monroe in the biopic about Yves Montand that the French director Christophe Ruggia was about to make.

The car had stopped for several minutes at the Crown Car Wash on West Pico Boulevard (Hollywood).

The driver was filling up the tank with petrol.

Suddenly, her attention was attracted to a little girl with caramel-coloured skin and golden hair in curls like springs. She was jumping for joy in puddles of water. She burst into laughter at the sight of a young man drenched with water who was going through the car-wash rollers while sitting on a child's bike.

A young man with very attractive eyes who resembled Ryan Gosling, only better-looking.

She got out of the car and the garage mechanic saw her. He looked at her for a long time, smiling; it was a very sweet smile.

Then he turned his head away, turned away from her entirely, leaving the perfect body there while he moved off and disappeared behind the car-wash rollers, as if swallowed up by a wave.

Acknowledgements

Infinite thanks to Karina Hocine and Claire Silve. You are my wings and a favourable wind.

To Emmanuelle Allibert and Laurence Barrère, who know how to touch hearts in order to open eyes.

To Eva Bredin who possessed the beautiful gift of being able to make words travel round the world.

To Olivia, Lydie and Véronique, my fairies.

To the journalists and booksellers who helped *The List of My Desires* follow the path to the stars.

To Philippe Dorey, the band at 17 rue Jacob, and all their representatives.

To all the readers who have been encouraging me for a long time and who are authors themselves, of marvellous letters – like little suns on a grey day, lifebelts on a stormy day.

And finally to Dana, the last person I will see.

Enjoy what you've read?
Turn over for the first chapter of
Grégoire Delacourt's
The List of My Desires.

We're always telling ourselves lies.

For instance, I know I'm not pretty. I don't have blue eyes, the kind in which men gaze at their own reflection, eyes in which they want to drown so that I'll dive in to rescue them. I don't have the figure of a model, I'm more the cuddly sort – well . . . plump. The sort who takes up a seat and a half. A man of medium height won't be able to get his arms all the way round me. I don't move with the grace of a woman to whom men whisper sweet nothings, punctuated by sighs . . . no, not me. I get brief, forthright comments. The bare bones of desire, nothing to embellish them, no comfortable padding.

I know all that.

All the same, when Jo isn't home I sometimes go up

to our bedroom and stand in front of the long mirror in our wardrobe – I must remind Jo to fix it to the wall before it squashes me flat one of these days while I'm in the midst of my *contemplation*.

Then I close my eyes and I undress, gently, the way no one has ever undressed me. I always feel a little cold; I shiver. When I'm entirely naked, I wait a little while before opening my eyes. I enjoy that moment. My mind wanders. I dream. I imagine the beautiful paintings of languid bodies in the art books that used to lie around my parents' house, and later I think of the more graphic bodies you see pictured in magazines.

Then I gently open my eyes, as if lifting the lids in slow motion.

I look at my body, my black eyes, my small breasts, my plump spare tyre, my forest of black hair, I think I look beautiful, and I swear that, in that moment, I really *am* beautiful, very beautiful even.

My beauty makes me profoundly happy. Tremendously strong.

It makes me forget unpleasant things. The haberdashery shop, which is quite boring.

The chit-chat of Danièle and Françoise, the twins who run the Coiff'Esthétique hair salon next door to my shop, and their obsession with playing the lottery. My beauty makes me forget the things that always stay the same. Like an uneventful life. Like this dreary town, no airport, a grey place – there's no escape from it and no one ever comes here, no heart-throb, no white knight on his white horse.

Arras. Population 42,000, 4 hypermarkets, 11 supermarkets, 4 fast-food outlets, a few medieval streets, a plaque in the Rue du Miroir-de-Venise telling passers-by and anyone who may have forgotten that Eugène-François Vidocq, an early private eye, was born here on 24 July 1775. And then there's my haberdashery shop.

Naked and beautiful in front of the mirror, I feel as if I'd only have to beat my arms in the air and I could fly away, light and graceful. As if my body might join the bodies in the art books lying about my childhood home. And then it would be as beautiful as them. Definitely.

But I never dare try.

The sound of Jo downstairs always takes me by surprise. It tears the silk of my dream. I get dressed again double quick. Shadows cover the clarity of my skin. I know about the wonderful beauty beneath my clothes, but Jo never sees it.

He did once tell me I was beautiful. That was over twenty years ago, when I was little more than twenty. I was wearing a pretty blue dress with a gilt belt, a fake touch of Dior about it; he wanted to sleep with me. He complimented me on my nice clothes.

So you see, we always tell ourselves lies.

Because love would never stand up to the truth.

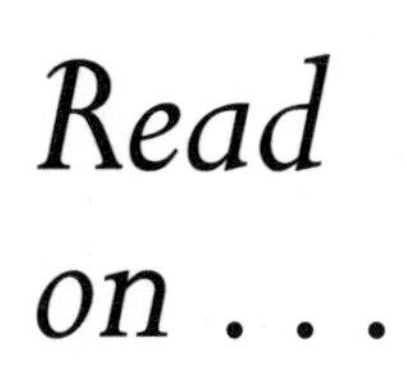

Read on . . .

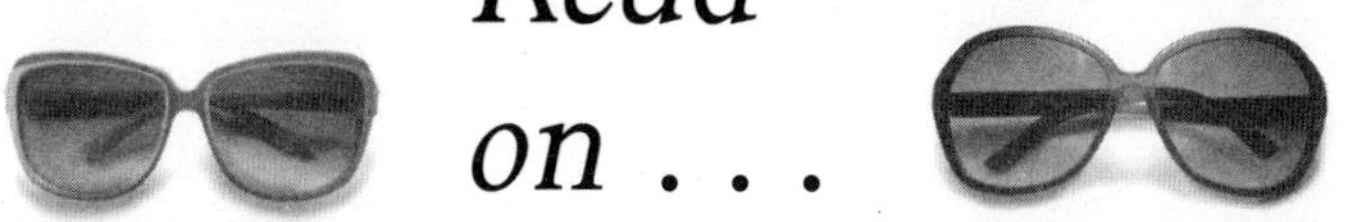

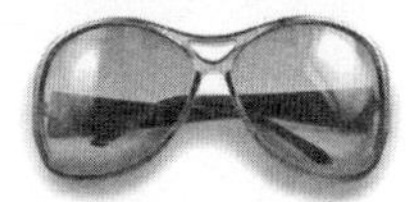
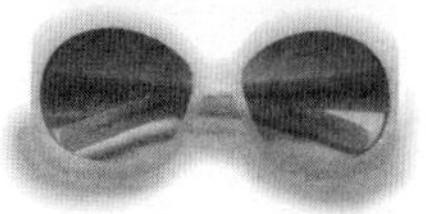

In conversation with Grégoire Delacourt

Q: *The First Thing You See* is a highly original love story. Where did your inspiration for the novel come from?

A: My inspiration came from an article in a French women's magazine which stated that one in two women aged fifteen to twenty-five was considering some form of cosmetic surgery. It made me wonder what we have done – or haven't done – to cause our children not to like themselves, even before they have come into their own. Because at fifteen – and I should know, having three daughters of my own – a person isn't yet 'finished'. So I began to explore the obsession with appearance that makes girls want to conform to certain criteria, and boys believe that those criteria define the only possible form of beauty. In the end, I wrote a book about desire, and the desire for love. At one point, the heroine asks her lover, 'Would you love me even if I didn't have this body?' It was the response to this question that I was searching for.

Q: Arthur's love of poetry, of Jean Follain in particular, permeates the novel. Why did you choose to have a protagonist with this interest? Did you draw inspiration from Follain's work?

A: Through poetry, I wanted to give Arthur other words with which to see the world, to feel things, and above all to discover the precise and precious vocabulary of love – so very different from the

abbreviated, coded language that is used today in text messages, Twitter and so on (a language that is often brutal and vulgar). Arthur's encounter with poetry is an encounter with the rich language of sensations; it gives him a key that allows him to approach the truth. A Canadian poet once said that poetry does not explain, but that it gives you an inkling. I love the immense possibilities this idea offers. And yes, I was overwhelmed by the work of Jean Follain when I discovered it at the age of eighteen. It is accessible poetry, a world away from that of the romantics or the depressed; an everyday kind of poetry. And that's what poetry should be, that is where it is really useful. In life, not in books.

Q: A major theme of the novel is the search for identity and the need for acceptance of one's true self. But Jeanine's nigh-exact physical resemblance to Scarlett takes this to an extreme – is it possible for Jeanine to have an identity devoid of Scarlett?

A: One of the biggest problems is when the person we appear to be doesn't match the person we actually are. Jeanine is mistaken for someone else (in this case Scarlett Johansson), but more than this, it is her 'sex appeal', her sensuality, that people see first, and which distorts the way people view her. Her biggest difficulty – as it is for millions of people – is to be loved for who she is, that is, for the kind of thing you can't see at first glance: her fundamental essence as a human being. And it's hard. The codes imposed on us by fashion, cinema, advertising skew everything. But I am an incurable romantic, so yes, I do think that she would be able to achieve an identity without Scarlett.

Q: Arthur is obsessed with Scarlett Johansson – his relationship with Jeanine was never going to have a happy ending, was it?

A: I don't think Arthur is obsessed with Scarlett. He is, like most men, attracted to the body of this woman, as those before him were to Marilyn Monroe or Sophia Loren. He has grown up in a world of 'appearances': steeped in a culture of images that not only shapes the way we look at the world, but also ideas around the body, and the body itself. As a novelist, I liked the notion of offering him one of the most beautiful women in the world. What would happen next? What would you do if such a woman suddenly rang your doorbell? You certainly wouldn't show off. You'd learn to look beyond appearances because suddenly you would find yourself face to face with a real person, not an image. That is what Arthur is going to learn, through poetry and through Jeanine's pain. Beauty can be a burden, you know. I think their relationship could have had a happy ending, but in the end I wanted to write a tragedy, a kind of modern *Romeo and Juliet*; it is because there is a sacrifice that the myth exists.

Q: Who are your favourite writers?

A: They change all the time! Nick Hornby. Edith Wharton. Hubert Selby. Jr. Jussi Adler Olsen. Lorraine Fouchet and her touching novel *Entre Ciel et Lou* . . .

Q: The next of your novels to be published in English is very different! Would you like to tell us briefly what it is about?

A: Photograph albums are always full of happy people. Smiles. Promises. Love. Good times. Happy holidays. You never see a shadow on a lung. A wound. A betrayal. A woman crying. You only see the happiness. So I decided to find out what the family of Antoine, my main character, had not put inside their album.

For Discussion

- What is your first reaction to Arthur Dreyfuss? Does your attitude toward him change throughout the novel?

- 'She was a chimera, a dream. There were respectable clinics where blades cut other faces to look like hers. Scalpels carved bodies, reshaping them in her image: big breasts, small waist. Jeanine Foucamprez brought unhappiness to men who couldn't possess her and women who didn't resemble her.' (pp 80-81)

  To what extent does *The First Thing You See* reflect our modern, celebrity-obsessed society? Does the author draw any judgements about the values of such a society?

- The male gaze is a prominent feature in *The First Thing You See*. Is the entire book simply a fantasy? Why, or why not?

- How did the title of this novel prepare you for the book? What was the first thing you saw in the novel?

- Did your impressions change when you read on, and looked beneath the surface?

- Discuss how Jeanine behaves when she is alone with Arthur, and then when she is in public. What differences do you notice?

- 'We ought to be seen as we see ourselves: in the kindly light of our self-esteem.' (p116)

  Why can this never be so?

- Arthur had a traumatic childhood. What effect has this had on him and how does he come to terms with it?

- Poetry, that of Jean Follain in particular, is very important to Arthur and figures prominently in his life. What does this tell us about him?

- Do you think Arthur and Jeanine could have been happy? What would that scenario have looked like for each of them?

- Is this a feminist novel?

Turn over to read an extract from
Grégoire Delacourt's next novel

We Only Saw Happiness

Antoine's parents fell in love at first sight. But they quickly realised that true love means more than furtive glances. Married too young, and with three small children, Antoine's mother retreats into a world of Sagan novels and cigarette smoke, abandoning the family when Antoine's sister dies. He grows up with a distant father, his only respite the tenderness he shares with his surviving sister.

Then Antoine meets Natalie, the woman of his dreams. They have two children and Antoine thrives in his work for an insurance company, investigating claims to reduce his firm's pay-outs. But soon Natalie drifts away from him, beginning an affair, and Antoine loses his job when he lets his heart overrule his head. Driven to despair, he does something unspeakable. Antoine's journey to come to terms with the terrible thing he has done will take him across seas and continents, deep into his own heart and the hearts of others, as he is forced to question what a life is really worth.

Available from W&N from October 2016

A life, and I was well placed to know, is worth between thirty and forty thousand euros.

A life. The cervix finally dilated to ten centimetres, breath coming short, birth, blood, tears, joy, pain; first bath, first teeth, first steps; new words, falling off a bike, braces from the dentist, the fear of tetanus; jokes, cousins, holidays, allergies to cat hair; tantrums, sweets, cavities; lies, sidelong glances, laughter, wonder, scarlet fever, gangly bodies shooting out in every direction, too-big ears, breaking voices, erections, partners, girls, blackhead remover, betrayals, doing good, wanting to change the world and kill the bastards, all the bastards; hangovers, shaving foam; heartache, love, wanting to die, the Baccalauréat, uni, romantic novels, the Stones, rock 'n' roll, drugs, curiosity, first job, first pay packet, painting the town red to celebrate it, getting engaged, getting married, cheating for the first

time, loving again, the need for love, the sweetness it arouses, nostalgia, the sudden speeding up of time, a shadow on the right lung, difficulty urinating in the morning, new embraces, skin, the texture of that skin, a suspect mole, tremors, savings, the warmth we seek, planning for afterwards, when they will be grown up, when we shall be two again, travels, blue oceans, blood-and-sand cocktails in the bar of a hotel with an unpronounceable name, in Mexico or some such place; a smile, clean sheets, the smell of freshness, together again, a prick as hard as stone, a headstone; a life.

It's worth between thirty and forty thousand euros if you get run over.

Twenty or twenty-five thousand if you're a child.

A little more than a hundred thousand if you're in a plane that falls from the sky, taking you and two hundred and twenty-seven other lives.

How much were ours worth?

*

I remember our delight the day you were born. You arrived three years after Joséphine. Nathalie seemed to have a second happy pregnancy. In the last three months she stopped going out in the afternoon, preferring the calm, cool peace of our house. In the last few weeks, she decided to repaint the kitchen, and then the bedrooms. We looked like the perfect young family, something out of a magazine, in shades of marshmallow pink. In photos from that time, Joséphine is putting cuddly toys in the cot, ready for her little brother. Joséphine is hugging her mother's big tummy. Joséphine is drawing and painting pictures, getting lots of welcome presents ready. Joséphine is doing a handstand in the sitting room. Playing mummies and babies with a doll. Joséphine is beautiful. Nathalie is planting hyacinth bulbs in our little garden. Nathalie, laughing, is showing her breasts, which are three times their usual size. Nathalie is blowing me a kiss. In our kitchen my father is smiling, his wife is holding his hand; Nathalie had made sea bass baked in a thyme and salt crust, and the fish was overdone. We don't see the fish being cooked in the photographs. We don't see the insincere compliments: *the sea bass was just perfect*. We see our new car. We see me standing next to the new car, looking like an idiot. We see the Barbie tricycle. We see Joséphine and Nathalie in the bath. We see Anna and her husband Thomas in our little garden beside a wilting hyacinth. We don't see my mother. We don't see the lies. We don't see the baby that Nathalie hadn't wanted to keep a year earlier, because she wasn't sure she would always love me. We don't see that love of ours, brief but infinite, vast and tragic. We don't see the tears I would shed back then. The nights I spent on the sofa. The insomnia that plagued me. The danger brewing at that time. The wild beast awakening.

We only saw happiness.

Tarry a little longer in France . . .

Money can buy you freedom. But what about happiness?

When Jocelyne looks at herself in the mirror, she sees a middle-aged, married woman who runs a dressmaking shop in a small provincial French town and lives a very ordinary existence. But what happened to all those dreams she had when she was 17?

Then she wins millions on the lottery and has the chance to change her life for ever. So why does she find herself reluctant to accept the money? To help her decide what to do, she begins to compile a list of her heart's desires, never suspecting for one moment that the decision might be taken out of her hands . . .

'As beautifully written as it is heart-breaking' *Stylist*

Available now from W&N in paperback, ebook and audio